WiLLiAM AT CHRiSTMAS

Richmal Crompton was born in Lancashire in 1890. The first story about William Brown appeared in *Home* magazine in 1919, and the first collection of William stories was published in book form three years later. In all, thirty-eight William books were published, the last one in 1970, after Richmal Crompton's death.

'Probably the funniest, toughest children's books ever written'
The Sunday Times on the Just William series

'Richmal Crompton's creation [has] been famed for his cavalier attitude to life and those who would seek to circumscribe his enjoyment of it ever since he first appeared'
The Guardian

Books available in the

Just William 100th anniversary edition series

Just William

More William

William Again

William the Outlaw

William at Christmas

Richmal Crompton
WiLLiAM
AT CHRiSTMAS

100 YEARS

Foreword by Julia Donaldson

Illustrated by Thomas Henry

MACMILLAN CHILDREN'S BOOKS

First published in 1995 as *Just William at Christmas* by Macmillan Children's Books

This edition published 2022 by Macmillan Children's Books
an imprint of Pan Macmillan
The Smithson, 6 Briset Street, London EC1M 5NR
EU representative: Macmillan Publishers Ireland Ltd, 1st Floor,
The Liffey Trust Centre, 117–126 Sheriff Street Upper
Dublin 1, D01 YC43
Associated companies throughout the world
www.panmacmillan.com

ISBN 978-1-5290-7691-2

All stories copyright © Edward Ashbee and Catherine Massey
This selection copyright © Edward Ashbee and Catherine Massey 1995
Foreword copyright © Julia Donaldson 2015
Illustrations copyright © Thomas Henry Fisher Estate

1 3 5 7 9 8 6 4 2

A CIP catalogue record for this book is available from the British Library.

Printed and bound by CPI Group (UK) Ltd, Croydon CR0 4YY

MIX
Paper | Supporting
responsible forestry
FSC® C116313

CONTENTS

FOREWORD

I was eleven – William's own age – when I started collecting the books about him. Unlike William, I was only eleven for one year. William is *always* eleven. The stories in *William at Christmas* are taken from different books, describing many different Christmases, so in theory he would be in his teens or twenties in the last story, but, just like Peter Pan, he never grows up.

William was my childhood hero. I was a town child, and I think what first attracted me to the stories was the country setting. I loved the idea of roaming woods and fields unsupervised, with a dog to explore rabbit holes, keepers to run away from, and an old barn where you could meet and plot and light fires. But once I was hooked on the books, what most appealed to me was William's way of talking – and, in particular, arguing. I liked the way he was always 'snorting sardonically' and I used to imitate his heavy sarcasm and righteous indignation: 'Huh! I like that!'

became my favourite exclamation, just as it was his.

Christmas is a time that William looks forward to with 'mingled feelings'. On the plus side there is the turkey, the trifle, the crackers and the pantomimes, but offset against these are all the visiting relations ('Aunts are the worst'), with their curious taste in presents. William and his friends, the Outlaws, pour scorn on the unwelcome history books, pencil cases and ties they are so often given. They yearn instead for mouth organs, airguns, sweets and pirate stories. So part of their Christmas ritual is to check where the presents are hidden, investigate them and then decide whether to hide them in the hope of being given money instead, or to bear their fate with resignation.

However, even the overabundance of prim aunts cannot dampen William's spirits for long. He is soon to be found singing 'Christians Awake!' very loudly and out of tune, and he is always ready to embark on a new adventure. The stories in this book illustrate the wide range of his ambitions. Whether he has decided to be an animal in a pantomime or an Arab in the desert, to play the trumpet or to cast out deceit, his enthusiasm is enormous. 'I bet I'll be the best elephant stuffer in the world by the time I've finished. You only need a bit more stuffin' for an elephant than what you do for a caterpillar, that's all.' His imagination is equally boundless: a wheelbarrow can be a fortress one minute, a wagon the next and then be converted into a cave or a mountain top or even a 'mortally wounded chieftain'.

And even though William's schemes invariably go wrong, his self-confidence is never seriously dented. The gadget he has unsuccessfully tried to take apart and put together must have something wrong with it, or the rat he has tried to stuff must have been a poor specimen, that's all.

Although William and the Outlaws wreak havoc and are the despair of their families and Sunday-School teachers, they are not in fact remotely bad. On the contrary, their escapades are often the result of the best intentions, and when penniless one of their main regrets is that they are unable to buy their mothers something nice for Christmas.

The stories are adventurous and touching, but above all they are funny. Rereading them I found myself laughing aloud when William, in an attempt to appear saintly, assumes his 'most expressionless expression', and when, mistaken for a Martian, he decides to act the part and comes out with 'Flam gobba manxy pop gebboo'.

If you've been given this book for Christmas – or if, like William, you have cunningly swapped around a couple of labels and received it instead of a book about the Kings and Queens of England – you are in for a treat.

Julia Donaldson

CHAPTER 1

A BUSY DAY

William awoke and rubbed his eyes. It was Christmas Day – the day to which he had looked forward with mingled feelings for twelve months. It was a jolly day, of course – presents and turkey and crackers and staying up late. On the other hand, there were generally too many relations about, too much was often expected of one, the curious taste displayed by people who gave one presents often marred one's pleasure.

He looked round his bedroom expectantly. On the wall, just opposite the bed, was a large illuminated card hanging by a string from a nail – 'A Busy Day is a Happy Day'. That had not been there the day before. Brightly-coloured roses and forget-me-nots and honeysuckle twined round all the words. William hastily thought over the three aunts staying in the house, and put it down to Aunt Lucy. He looked at it with a doubtful frown. He distrusted the sentiment.

A copy of *Portraits of our Kings and Queens* he put aside as beneath contempt. *Things a Boy Can Do* was more promising. *Much* more promising. After inspecting a penknife, a pocket-compass, and a pencil-box (which shared the fate of *Portraits of our Kings and Queens*), William returned to *Things a Boy Can Do*. As he turned the pages, his face lit up.

He leapt lightly out of bed and dressed. Then he began to arrange his own gifts to his family. For his father he had bought a bottle of highly-coloured sweets, for his elder brother Robert (aged nineteen) he had expended a vast sum of money on a copy of *The Pirates of the Bloody Hand*. These gifts had cost him much thought. The knowledge that his father never touched sweets, and that Robert professed scorn of pirate stories, had led him to hope that the recipients of his gifts would make no objection to the unobtrusive theft of them by their recent donor in the course of the next few days. For his grown-up sister Ethel he had bought a box of coloured chalks. That also might come in useful later. Funds now had been running low, but for his mother he had bought a small cream jug which, after fierce bargaining, the man had let him have at half-price because it was cracked.

Singing 'Christians Awake!' at the top of his lusty young voice, he went along the landing, putting his gifts outside the doors of his family, and pausing to yell 'Happy Christmas' as he did so. From within he was greeted in each case by muffled groans.

He went downstairs into the hall, still singing. It was earlier than he thought – just five o'clock. The maids were not down yet. He switched on lights recklessly, and discovered that he was not the only person in the hall. His four-year-old cousin Jimmy was sitting on the bottom step in an attitude of despondency, holding an empty tin.

Jimmy's mother had influenza at home, and Jimmy and his small sister Barbara were in the happy position of spending Christmas with relations, but immune from parental or maternal interference.

'They've gotten out,' said Jimmy, sadly. 'I got 'em for presents yesterday, an' they've gotten out. I've been feeling for 'em in the dark, but I can't find 'em.'

'What?' said William.

'Snails. Great big suge ones wiv great big suge shells. I put 'em in a tin for presents an' they've gotten out an' I've gotten no presents for nobody.'

He relapsed into despondency.

William surveyed the hall.

'They've got out right enough!' he said, sternly. 'They've got out right *enough*. Jus' look at our hall! Jus' look at our clothes! They've got out *right* enough.'

Innumerable slimy iridescent trails shone over hats, and coats, and umbrellas, and wallpaper.

'Huh!' grunted William, who was apt to overwork his phrases. 'They got *out* right enough.'

He looked at the tracks again and brightened. Jimmy was frankly delighted.

'Oo! Look!' he cried. 'Oo *funny*!'

William's thoughts flew back to his bedroom wall – 'A Busy Day is a Happy Day'.

'Let's clean it up!' he said. 'Let's have it all nice an' clean for when they come down. We'll be busy. You tell me if you feel happy when we've done. It might be true wot it says, but I don't like the flowers messin' all over it.'

Investigation in the kitchen provided them with a large

pail of water and scrubbing-brush each.

For a long time they worked in silence. They used plenty of water. When they had finished the trails were all gone. Each soaked garment on the hatstand was sending a steady drip on to the already flooded floor. The wallpaper was sodden. With a feeling of blankness they realised that there was nothing else to clean.

It was Jimmy who conceived the exquisite idea of dipping his brush in the bucket and sprinkling William with water. A scrubbing-brush is in many ways almost as good as a hose. Each had a pail of ammunition. Each had a good-sized brush. During the next few minutes they experienced purest joy. Then William heard threatening movements above, and decided hastily that the battle must cease.

'Backstairs,' he said shortly. 'Come on.'

Marking their tracks by a running stream of water, they crept up the backstairs.

But two small boys soaked to the skin could not disclaim all knowledge of a flooded hall.

William was calm and collected when confronted with a distracted mother.

'We was tryin' to clean up,' he said. 'We found all snail

marks an' we was tryin' to clean up. We was tryin' to help. You said so last night, you know, when you was talkin' to me. You said to *help*. Well, I thought it was helpin' to try an' clean up. You can't clean up with water an' not get wet – not if you do it prop'ly. You said to try an' make Christmas Day happy for other folks and then I'd be happy. Well, I don't know as I'm very happy,' he said, bitterly, 'but I've been workin' hard enough since early this mornin'. I've been workin',' he went on pathetically. His eye wandered to the notice on his wall. 'I've been *busy* all right, but it doesn't make me *happy* – not jus' now,' he added, with memories of the rapture of the fight. That certainly must be repeated some time. Buckets of water and scrubbing-brushes. He wondered he'd never thought of that before.

William's mother looked down at his dripping form.

'Did you get all that water with just cleaning up the snail marks?' she said.

William coughed and cleared his throat. 'Well,' he said, deprecatingly, 'most of it. I think I got most of it.'

'If it wasn't Christmas Day . . .' she went on darkly.

William's spirits rose. There was certainly something to be said for Christmas Day.

It was decided to hide the traces of the crime as far as possible from William's father. It was felt – and not without reason – that William's father's feelings of respect for the sanctity of Christmas Day might be overcome by his feelings of paternal ire.

Half an hour later William, dried, dressed, brushed, and chastened, descended the stairs as the gong sounded in a hall which was bare of hats and coats, and whose floor shone with cleanliness.

'And jus' to think,' said William, despondently, 'that it's only jus' got to brekfust time.'

William's father was at the bottom of the stairs. William's father frankly disliked Christmas Day.

'Good morning, William,' he said, 'and a happy Christmas, and I hope it's not too much to ask of you that on this relation-infested day one's feelings may be harrowed by you as little as possible. And why the deu—dickens they think it necessary to wash the hall floor before breakfast, Heaven only knows!'

William coughed, a cough meant to be a polite mixture of greeting and deference. William's face was a study in holy innocence. His father glanced at him suspiciously. There were certain expressions of William's that he distrusted.

William entered the dining-room morosely. Jimmy's sister Barbara – a small bundle of curls and white frills – was already beginning her porridge.

'Goo' mornin'',' she said, politely. 'Did you hear me cleanin' my teef?'

He crushed her with a glance.

He sat eating in silence till everyone had come down, and Aunts Jane, Evangeline and Lucy were consuming porridge with that mixture of festivity and solemnity that they felt the occasion demanded.

Then Jimmy entered, radiant, with a tin in his hand.

'Got presents,' he said, proudly. 'Got presents, lots of presents.'

He deposited on Barbara's plate a worm which Barbara promptly threw at his face. Jimmy looked at her reproachfully and proceeded to Aunt Evangeline. Aunt Evangeline's gift was a centipede – a live centipede that ran gaily off the tablecloth on to Aunt Evangeline's lap before anyone could stop it. With a yell that sent William's father to the library with his hands to his ears, Aunt Evangeline leapt to her chair and stood with her skirts held to her knees.

'Help! Help!' she cried. 'The horrible boy! Catch it! Kill it!'

Jimmy gazed at her in amazement, and Barbara looked with interest at Aunt Evangeline's long expanse of shin.

'*My* legs isn't like *your* legs,' she said pleasantly and conversationally. 'My legs is knees.'

It was some time before order was restored, the centipede killed, and Jimmy's remaining gifts thrown out of the window. William looked across the table at Jimmy with respect in his eye. Jimmy, in spite of his youth, was an acquaintance worth cultivating. Jimmy was eating porridge unconcernedly.

Aunt Evangeline had rushed from the room when the slaughter of the centipede had left the coast clear, and refused to return. She carried on a conversation from the top of the stairs.

'When that horrible child has gone, I'll come in. He may have insects concealed on his person. And someone's been dropping water all over these stairs. They're *damp*!'

'Dear, dear!' murmured Aunt Jane, sadly.

Jimmy looked up from his porridge.

'How was I to know she didn't like insecks?' he said,

aggrievedly. '*I* like 'em.'

William's mother's despair was only tempered by the fact that this time William was not the culprit. To William also it was a novel sensation. He realised the advantages of a fellow criminal.

After breakfast peace reigned. William's father went out for a walk with Robert. The aunts sat round the drawing-room fire talking and doing crochet-work. In this consists the whole art and duty of aunthood. *All* aunts do crochet-work.

They had made careful inquiries about the time of the service.

'You needn't worry,' had said William's mother. 'It's at ten-thirty, and if you go to get ready when the clock in the library strikes ten it will give you heaps of time.'

Peace . . . calm . . . quiet. Mrs Brown and Ethel in the kitchen supervising the arrangements for the day. The aunts in the drawing-room discussing over their crochet-work the terrible way in which their sisters had brought up their children. That, also, is a necessary part of aunt-hood.

Time slipped by happily and peacefully. Then William's mother came into the drawing-room.

'I thought you were going to church,' she said.

'We are. The clock hasn't struck.'

'But – it's eleven o'clock!'

There was a gasp of dismay.

'The clock never struck!'

Indignantly they set off to the library. Peace and quiet reigned also in the library. On the floor sat William and Jimmy gazing with frowns of concentration at an open page of *Things a Boy Can Do*. Around them lay, most indecently exposed, the internal arrangements of the library clock.

'William! You *wicked* boy!'

William raised a frowning face.

'It's not put together right,' he said. 'It's not been put together right all this time. We're makin' it right now. It must have wanted mendin' for ever so long. *I* dunno how it's been goin' at all. It's lucky we found it out. It's put together wrong. I guess it's *made* wrong. It's goin' to be a lot of trouble to us to put it right, an' we can't do much when you're all standin' in the light. We're very busy – workin' at tryin' to mend this ole clock for you all.'

'Clever,' said Jimmy, admiringly. 'Mendin' the clock. *Clever!*'

AROUND THEM LAY, MOST INDECENTLY EXPOSED, THE
INTERNAL ARRANGEMENTS OF THE LIBRARY CLOCK.

'William!' groaned his mother. 'You've ruined the clock. What *will* your father say?'

'Well, the cog wheels was wrong,' said William doggedly. 'See? An' this ratchet-wheel isn't on the pawl prop'ly – not like what this book says it ought to be. Seems we've got to take it all to pieces to get it right. Seems to me the person wot made this clock didn't know much about clock-making. Seems to me—'

'Be *quiet*, William!'

'We was be quietin' 'fore you came in,' said Jimmy severely. 'You 'sturbed us.'

'Leave it just as it is, William,' said his mother.

'You don't *unnerstand*,' said William with the excitement of the fanatic. 'The cog wheel an' the ratchet ought to be put on the arbor different. See, this is the cog wheel. Well, it oughtn't to be like wot it was. It was put on all *wrong*. Well, we was mendin' it. An' we was doin' it for *you*,' he ended, bitterly, 'jus' to help an' – to – to make other folks happy. It makes folks happy havin' clocks goin' right, anyone would *think*. But if you *want* your clocks put together wrong, *I* don't care.'

He picked up his book and walked proudly from the

room followed by the admiring Jimmy.

'William,' said Aunt Lucy patiently, as he passed. 'I don't want to say anything unkind, and I hope you won't remember all your life that you have completely spoilt this Christmas Day for me.'

'Oh, dear!' murmured Aunt Jane, sadly.

William, with a look before which she should have sunk into the earth, answered shortly that he didn't think he would.

During the midday dinner the grown-ups, as is the foolish fashion of grown-ups, wasted much valuable time in the discussion of such futilities as the weather and the political state of the nation. Aunt Lucy was still suffering and aggrieved.

'I can go this evening, of course,' she said, 'but it's not quite the same. The morning service is different. Yes, please, dear – *and* stuffing. Yes, I'll have a little more turkey, too. And, of course, the vicar may not preach tonight. That makes such a difference. The gravy on the potatoes, please. It's almost the first Christmas I've not been in the morning. It seems quite to have spoilt the day for me.'

She bent on William a glance of gentle reproach. William was quite capable of meeting adequately that or any other glance, but at present he was too busy for minor hostilities. He was *extremely* busy. He was doing his utmost to do full justice to a meal that only happens once a year.

'William,' said Barbara pleasantly, 'I can *dweam*. Can you?'

He made no answer.

'Answer your cousin, William,' said his mother.

He swallowed, then spoke plaintively. 'You always say not to talk with my mouth full,' he said.

'You could speak when you've finished the mouthful.'

'No. 'Cause I want to fill it again then,' said William, firmly.

'Dear, *dear*!' murmured Aunt Jane.

This was Aunt Jane's usual contribution to any conversation.

He looked coldly at the three pairs of horrified aunts' eyes around him, then placidly continued his meal.

Mrs Brown hastily changed the subject of conversation. The art of combining the duties of mother and hostess is sometimes a difficult one.

Christmas afternoon is a time of rest. The three aunts withdrew from public life. Aunt Lucy found a book of sermons in the library and retired to her bedroom with it.

'It's the next best thing, I think,' she said with a sad glance at William.

William was beginning definitely to dislike Aunt Lucy.

'Please'm,' said the cook an hour later, 'the mincing machine's disappeared.'

'Disappeared?' said William's mother, raising her hand to her head.

'Clean gone'm. 'Ow'm I to get the supper'm? You said as 'ow I could get it done this afternoon so as to go to church this evening. I can't do nuffink with the mincing machine gone.'

'I'll come and look.'

They searched every corner of the kitchen, then William's mother had an idea. William's mother had not been William's mother for eleven years without learning many things. She went wearily up to William's bedroom.

William was sitting on the floor. Open beside him was 'Things a Boy Can Do'. Around him lay various parts of the mincing machine. His face was set and strained in mental

16

and physical effort. He looked up as she entered.

'It's a funny kind of mincin' machine,' he said crushingly. 'It's not got enough parts. It's *made* wrong—'

'Do you know,' she said, slowly, 'that we've all been looking for that mincing machine for the last half-hour?'

'No,' he said without much interest. 'I di'n't. I'd have told you I was mendin' it if you'd told me you was lookin' for it. It's *wrong*,' he went on aggrievedly. 'I can't make anything with it. Look! It says in my book "How to make a model railway signal with parts of a mincing machine." Listen! It says "Borrow a mincing machine from your mother—"'

'Did you borrow it?' said Mrs Brown.

'Yes. Well, I've got it, haven't I? I went all the way down to the kitchen for it.'

'Who lent it to you?'

'No one *lent* it me. I *borrowed* it. I thought you'd like to see a model railway signal. I thought you'd be interested. Anyone would think anyone would be interested in seein' a railway signal made out of a mincin' machine.'

His tone implied that the dullness of people in general was simply beyond him. 'An' you haven't got a right sort of mincin' machine. It's wrong. Its parts are the wrong shape. I've been hammerin' them, tryin' to make them right, but they're *made* wrong.'

Mrs Brown was past expostulating. 'Take them all down to the kitchen to cook,' she said. 'She's waiting for them.'

On the stairs William met Aunt Lucy carrying her volume of sermons.

'It's not quite the same as the spoken word, William dear,' she said. 'It hasn't the *force*. The written word doesn't reach the *heart* as the spoken word does, but I don't want you to worry about it.'

William walked on as if he had not heard her.

It was Aunt Jane who insisted on the little entertainment after tea.

'I *love* to hear the dear children recite,' she said. 'I'm sure they all have some little recitation they can say.'

Barbara rose with shy delight to say her piece.

'Lickle bwown seed, lickle bwown bwother,*
And what, pway, are you goin' to be?
I'll be a poppy as white as my mother,
Oh, DO be a poppy like me!

A Busy Day

What, you'll be a sunflower? Oh, how I shall miss you
When you are golden and high!
But I'll send all the bees up to tiss you.
Lickle bwown bwother, good-bye!'

She sat down blushing, amid rapturous applause.

Next Jimmy was dragged from his corner. He stood up as one prepared for the worst, shut his eyes, and—

'Licklaxokindness lickledeedsolove –
make – thisearfanedenliketheeav'nabovethasalliknow,'

He gasped it all in one breath, and sat down panting.

This was greeted with slightly milder applause.

'Now, William!'

'I don't know any,' he said.

'Oh, you *do*,' said his mother. 'Say the one you learnt at school last term. Stand up, dear, and speak clearly.'

Slowly William rose to his feet.

'It was the schooner Hesperus that sailed the wintry sea,'

he began.

Here he stopped, coughed, cleared his throat, and began again.

'It was the schooner Hesperus that sailed the wintry sea.'

'Oh, get *on*!' muttered his brother, irritably.

'I can't get on if you keep talkin' to me,' said William sternly. 'How can I get on if you keep takin' all the time up, *sayin'* get on? I can't get on if you're talkin', can I?

'It was the Hesper Schoonerus that sailed the wintry sea an' I'm not going' on if Ethel's goin' to keep gigglin'. It's not a funny piece, an' if she's goin' on gigglin' like that I'm not sayin' any more of it.'

'Ethel, dear!' murmured Mrs Brown, reproachfully. Ethel turned her chair completely round and left her back only exposed to William's view. He glared at it suspiciously.

'Now, William, dear,' continued his mother, 'begin again and no one shall interrupt you.'

William again went through the preliminaries of coughing and clearing his throat.

'It was the schooner Hesperus that sailed the wintry seas.'

He stopped again, and slowly and carefully straightened his collar and smoothed back the lock of hair which was dangling over his brow.

'*The skipper had brought*—' prompted Aunt Jane, kindly.

William turned on her.

'IT WAS THE HESPER SCHOONERUS THAT SAILED
THE WINTRY SEA AN' I'M NOT GOIN' ON IF
ETHEL'S GOIN' TO KEEP GIGGLIN'.'

'I was *goin'* to say that if you'd left me alone,' he said. 'I was jus' thinkin'. I've got to think sometimes. I can't say off a great long pome like that without stoppin' to think sometimes, can I? I'll – I'll do a conjuring trick for you instead,' he burst out, desperately. 'I've learnt one from my book. I'll go an' get it ready.'

He went out of the room. Mr Brown took out his handkerchief and mopped his brow.

'May I ask,' he said patiently, 'how long this exhibition is to be allowed to continue?'

Here William returned, his pockets bulging. He held a large handkerchief in his hand.

'This is a handkerchief,' he announced. 'If anyone'd like to feel it to see if it's a real one, they can. Now I want a shilling.' He looked round expectantly, but no one moved, 'Or a penny would do,' he said, with a slightly disgusted air. Robert threw one across the room. 'Well, I put the penny into the handkerchief. You can see me do it, can't you? If anyone wants to come an' feel the penny is in the handkerchief, they can. Well,' he turned his back on them and took something out of his pocket. After a few contortions he turned round again, holding the handkerchief tightly. 'Now, you look close' – he went over to them – 'an' you'll see the shil— I mean, penny,' he looked scornfully at Robert, 'has changed to an egg. It's a real egg. If anyone thinks it isn't a real egg—'

But it *was* a real egg. It confirmed his statement by giving a resounding crack and sending a shining stream partly on to the carpet and partly on to Aunt Evangeline's black silk knee. A storm of reproaches burst out.

'First that horrible insect,' almost wept Aunt Evangeline, 'and then this messy stuff all over me. It's a good thing I don't live here. One day a year is enough . . . My nerves! . . .'

'Dear, dear!' said Aunt Jane.

'Fancy taking a new-laid *egg* for that,' said Ethel severely.

William was pale and indignant.

'Well, I did jus' what the book said to do. Look at it. It says: "Take an egg. Conceal it in the pocket." Well, I took an egg an' I concealed it in the pocket. Seems to me,' he said bitterly, 'seems to me this book isn't *Things a Boy Can Do*. It's Things a Boy Can't Do.'

Mr Brown rose slowly from his chair.

'You're just about right there, my son. Thank *you*,' he said with elaborate politeness, as he took the book from

William's reluctant hands and went over with it to a small cupboard in the wall. In this cupboard reposed an airgun, a bugle, a catapult, and a mouth organ, As he unlocked it to put the book inside, the fleeting glimpse of his confiscated treasures added to the bitterness of William's soul.

'On Christmas Day, too!'

While he was still afire with silent indignation Aunt Lucy returned from church.

'The vicar *didn't* preach,' she said. 'They say that this morning's sermon was beautiful. As I say, I don't want William to reproach himself, but I feel that he has deprived me of a very great treat.'

'*Nice* Willum!' murmured Jimmy sleepily from his corner.

As William undressed that night his gaze fell upon the flower-bedecked motto: 'A Busy Day is a Happy Day.'

'It's a story,' he said, indignantly. 'It's jus' a wicked ole story.'

CHAPTER 2

WiLLiAM ALL THE TiME

William WAS walking down the road, his hands in his pockets, his mind wholly occupied with the Christmas pantomime. He was going to the Christmas pantomime next week. His thoughts dwelt on rapturous memories of previous Christmas pantomimes – of *Puss in Boots*, of *Dick Whittington*, of *Red Riding Hood*. His mouth curved into a blissful smile as he thought of the funny man – inimitable funny man with his red nose and enormous girth. How William had roared every time he appeared! With what joy he had listened to his uproarious songs! But it was not the funny man to whom William had given his heart. It was to the animals. It was to the cat in *Puss in Boots*, the robins in *The Babes in the Wood*, and the wolf in *Red Riding Hood*. He wanted to be an animal in a pantomime. He was quite willing to relinquish his beloved future career of pirate in favour of that of animal in a pantomime. He wondered . . .

It was at this point that Fate, who often had a special eye on William, performed one of her lightning tricks.

A man in shirt-sleeves stepped out of the wood and looked anxiously up and down the road. Then he took out his watch and muttered to himself. William stood still and stared at him with frank interest. Then the man began to stare at William, first as if he didn't see him, and then as if he saw him.

'Would you like to be a bear for a bit?' he said.

William pinched himself. He seemed to be awake.

'A b-b-bear?' he queried, his eyes almost starting out of his head.

'Yes,' said the man irritably, 'a bear. B.E.A.R. bear, animal – zoo. Never heard of a bear?'

William pinched himself again. He seemed to be still awake.

'Yes,' he agreed as though unwilling to commit himself entirely. 'I've heard of a bear all right.'

'Come on, then,' said the man, looking once more at his

watch, once more up the road, once more down the road, then turning on his heel and walking quickly into the wood.

William followed, both mouth and eyes wide open. The man did not speak as he walked down the path. Then suddenly down a bend in the path they came upon a strange sight. There was a hut in a little clearing, and round the

SUDDENLY DOWN A BEND IN THE PATH THEY
CAME UPON A STRANGE SIGHT.

hut was clustered a group of curious people – a Father Christmas, holding his beard in one hand and a glass of ale in the other; a rather Goldilocks, in the act of having yellow powder lavishly applied to her face; several fairies and elves, sucking large and redolent peppermints; a ferocious, but depressed-looking giant, rubbing his hands together and complaining of the cold; and several other strange and incongruous figures. In front of the hut was a large species of camera with a handle, and behind stood a man smoking a pipe.

'Kid turned up?' he said.

William's guide shook his head.

'No,' he said, 'they've missed their train or lost their way, or evaporated, or got kidnapped or something, but this happened to be passing, and it looked the same size pretty near. What do you think?'

The man took his pipe from his mouth in order the better to concentrate his whole attention on William. He looked at William from his muddy boots to his untidy head. Then he reversed the operation, and looked from his untidy head to his muddy boots. Then he scratched his head.

'Seems on the big side for the middle one,' he said.

At this point a hullabaloo arose from behind the shed, and a small bear appeared, howling loudly.

'He tooken my bit of toffee,' yelled the bear in a very human voice.

'Aw, shut up!' said the man in his shirt-sleeves.

The small bear was followed by a large bear, protesting loudly.

'I gave him half'n mine 'n'e promised to give me half'n his' 'n' then he tried to eat it all'n'—'

'Aw, shut up!' repeated the man. Then he turned to William.

'All you gotter do,' he said, 'is to fix on the middle bear's suit an' do exactly what you're told, an' I'll give you five shillings at the end. See?'

'These roural places are a butiful chinge,' murmured Goldilocks' mother, darkening her eyebrows as she spoke. 'So calm and quart.'

'These Christmas shows,' grumbled the giant, flapping his arms vigorously, 'are the very devil.'

Here William found his voice. 'Crumbs!' he ejaculated. Then, feeling the expletive to be altogether inadequate to the occasion, quickly added: 'Gosh!'

'Take the kid round, someone,' said the shirt-sleeve man wearily, 'and fix on his togs, and let's get on with the show.'

Here a Fairy Queen appeared from behind the hut.

'I don't see how I'm possibly to go through with this here performance,' she said in a voice of plaintive suffering. 'I had toothache all last night—'

'If you think,' said the shirt-sleeve man, 'that you can hold up this blessed show for a twopenny-halfpenny toothache—'

'If you're going to be insulting—' said the Fairy Queen in shrill indignation.

'Aw, shut up!' said the shirt-sleeve man.

Here Father Christmas, who had finished his ale, led William into the hut. A bear's suit lay on a chair.

'The kid wot was to wear this not having turned up,' he said by way of explanation, 'and you by all accounts bein' willin' to oblige for a small consideration, we shall have to see what can be done. I suppose,' he added, 'you have no objection?'

'Me?' said William, whose eyes and mouth had grown more and more circular every minute. '*Me* – objection? Golly! I should think *not*.'

The little bear and the big bear surveyed him critically.

'He's too *big*,' said the little bear contemptuously.

'His hair's too long,' contributed the big bear.

'His face is too dirty.'

'His ears is too long.'

'His nose is too flat.'

'His head's too big.'

'His—'

William speedily and joyfully put an end to the duet and Father Christmas wearily disentangled the struggling mass.

'It may be a bit on the small side,' he conceded as he deposited the small bear upside down beneath the table, 'but we'll do what we can.'

Here the shirt-sleeve man appeared at the window.

'That's right,' he said kindly. 'Take all day about it. Don't hurry! We all enjoy hanging about and waiting for you.'

Father Christmas offered to retire from his post in favour of the shirt-sleeve man, and the shirt-sleeve man hastily retreated.

Then came the task of fitting William into the skin. It was not an easy task.

'You're bigger,' said Father Christmas, 'than what you look in the distance. Considerable.'

William could not stand quite upright in the skin, but by stooping slightly he could see and speak through the open mouth of the head. In an ecstasy of joy he pummelled the big bear, the little bear gladly joined in the fray and a furry ball of three struggling bears rolled out of the door of the hut.

The shirt-sleeve man rang a bell.

'After this somewhat lengthy interlude,' he said. 'By the way, may I inquire the name of our new friend?'

William proudly shouted his name through the aperture in the bear's head.

'Well, Billiam,' he said jocularly, 'do just what I tell you and you'll be all right. Now all clear off a minute, please. We've only a few scenes to do here.'

'Location,' he read from a paper in his hand, 'hut in wood. Enter fairies with Fairy Queen. Dance.'

'How I am expected to dance,' said the Fairy Queen bitterly, 'tortured by toothache, I can't think.'

'You don't dance with your teeth,' said the shirt-sleeve man unsympathetically. 'Let's go through it once before we turn on the machine. You've rehearsed it often enough. Now, come on.'

They danced a dance that made William gape in surprise and admiration, so dainty and airy was it.

'Enter Father Christmas,' went on the shirt-sleeve man.

'What I can't think,' said Father Christmas, fastening on his beard, 'is what a Father Christmas's doing in this effect.'

'Nor a giant,' said the giant sadly.

'It's for a Christmas show,' said the shirt-sleeve man. 'You've gotter have a Father Christmas in a Christmas show, or else how'd people know it's a Christmas show? And you've gotter have a giant in a fairy tale whether there is one in it or not.'

Father Christmas joined the dance – gave presents to all the fairies, then retired behind the hut to his private store of refreshment.

'Enter Goldilocks,' said the shirt-sleeve man. 'Now, where the dickens is that kid?'

Goldilocks, fair and rosy, appeared from behind a tree where she had been eating bananas.

She peered down the middle bear's mouth.

'It's a new one,' she said.

'The other hasn't turned up,' said the man. 'This is Billiam, who is taking on the middle one for the small consideration of five shillings.'

'He's put out his tongue at me,' she screamed in shrill indignation.

At this the big bear, whose adoration of Goldilocks was very obvious, closed with William, and Goldilocks' mother screamed shrilly.

The giant separated the two bears and Goldilocks came to the hut with an expression of patient suffering meant to represent intense physical weariness. She gave a start of joy at the sight of the hut, which apparently she did not see till she had almost passed it. She entered. She gave a second start of joy at the sight of three porridge plates. She tasted the first two and consumed the third. She wandered into the other room. She gave a third start of joy at the sight of three beds. She tried them all and went to sleep beautifully and realistically on the smallest. William was lost in admiration.

'Come on, bears,' said the man in shirt-sleeves. 'Billiam, walk between them. Don't jump. *Walk*. In at the door. That's right. Now, Billiam, look at your plate, then shake your head at the big bear.'

Trembling with joy, William obeyed. The big bear, in the privacy of the open mouth, put out his tongue at William with a hostile grimace. William returned it.

'Now to the little one,' said the man in shirt-sleeves. But William was still absorbed in the big one. Enraged by a particularly brilliant feat in the grimacing line which he felt he could not outshine, he put out a paw and tripped up the big bear's chair. The big bear promptly picked up a porridge plate and broke it on William's head. The little bear hurled himself ecstatically into the conflict. Father Christmas wearily returned to his work of separating them.

'If you aren't satisfied with your bonus,' said the shirt-sleeve man to William, 'take it out on me, not the scenery. You've just done about five shillings' worth of damage already. Now let's get on.'

The rest of the scene went off fairly well, but William was growing bored. It wasn't half such fun as he thought it would be. He wasn't feeling quite sure of his five shillings after those smashed plates. The only thing for which he felt a deep and lasting affection, from which he felt he could never endure to be parted, was his bear-skin. It was rather small and very hot, but it gave him a thrill of pleasure unlike

anything he had ever known before. He was a bear. He was
an animal in a pantomime. He began to dislike immensely
the shirt-sleeve man, and the hut, and the Fairy Queen, and
the giant, and all the rest of them, but he loved his bear
suit. It was while the giant was having a scene by himself
that the brilliant idea came to William. He was standing
behind a tree. No one was looking at him. He moved very
quietly further away. Still no one looked at him. He moved
yet further away and still no one looked at him. In a few
seconds he was leaping and bounding through the wood
alone in the world with the bear-skin. He was a bear. He
was a bear in a wood. He ran. He jumped. He turned head
over heels. He climbed a tree. He ran after a rabbit. He was
riotously, blissfully happy. He met a boy who fled from him
with echoing yells of terror, and to William it seemed as if
he had drunk of ecstasy's very fount. He ran on and on,
roaring occasionally, and occasionally rolling in the leaves.
Then something happened. He gave a particularly violent
jump and strained the skin which was already somewhat
tight. The skin did not burst, but the head came down
very far on to William's head and wedged itself tightly. He
could not see out of its open mouth now. He could just

see out of one of the eye holes, but only just. His mouth was wedged tightly in the head and he found he could not speak plainly. He put up his paws and pulled at the head to loosen it, but with no results. It was very tightly wedged. William's spirits drooped. It was all very well being a bear in a wood as long as one could change oneself to a boy at will. It was a very different thing being fastened to a bear-skin for life. He supposed that in time, if he went on

HE MET A BOY WHO FLED FROM HIM WITH YELLS OF
TERROR, AND TO WILLIAM IT SEEMED AS IF HE
HAD DRUNK IN ECSTASY'S VERY FOUNT.

growing to a man, he'd burst the bear-skin. On the other hand, he couldn't get to his mouth now, so he couldn't eat, and he'd not be able to grow at all. Starvation stared him in the face. He was hungry already. He decided to return home and throw himself on the mercy of his family. Then he remembered that his family were all out that afternoon. His mother was at a mothers' meeting at the Vicarage. He decided to go straight to the Vicarage. Perhaps the united efforts of the mothers of the village might succeed in getting his head off. He went out from the woods on to the road but was discouraged by the behaviour of a woman who was passing. She gave an unearthly yell, tore a leg of mutton from her basket, flung it at William's head, and ran for dear life down the road, screaming as she went. William, much depressed, returned to the woods and reached the Vicarage by a circuitous route. Feeling too shy to ring the bell and interview a housemaid in his present costume, he walked round the house to the French windows of the dining-room where the meeting was taking place. He stood pathetically in the doorway of the window.

'Mother,' he began plaintively in a muffled and almost inaudible voice, but it would have made little difference had

he spoken in his usual strident tones. The united scream of
the mother's meeting would have drowned it. Never in the
whole course of his life had William seen a room empty
so quickly. It was like magic. Almost before his plaintive
and muffled 'Mother' had left his lips, the room was empty.
Only two dozen overturned chairs, an overturned table,
and several broken ornaments marked the line of retreat.
The room was empty.

The entire mothers' meeting, headed by the vicar's
wife and the vicarage cook and housemaid, were dashing
down the main road of the village, screaming as they went.
William sadly surveyed the desolate scene before him and
retreated again to the woods. He leant against a tree and
considered the whole situation.

'Hello, Billiam!'

Turning his head to a curious angle and peering out of
one of the bear's eye-holes, he recognised Goldilocks.

'Hello!' he returned in a spiritless voice.

'Why did you run away?' she said.

'Dunno,' he said. 'I wanted the old skin. Wish I'd never
seed it.'

'You do talk funny,' she said. 'I can't hear what you say.'

NEVER IN THE WHOLE COURSE OF HIS LIFE HAD
WILLIAM SEEN A ROOM EMPTY SO QUICKLY.

And so far was William's spirit broken that he only sighed.

'I saw you going,' she went on, 'and I went after you, but you ran so fast that I lost you. Then I went round a bit by myself. I say, they won't be able to get on with the old thing without us. I heard them shouting for us. Isn't it fun? An' I heard some people screaming in the road. What was that?'

William sighed again. Then he shouted: 'Try'n pull my head loose. *Hard*.'

She complied. She pulled till William yelled again.

'You've nearly took my ears off,' he said angrily in his muffled, sepulchral voice.

But the head was wedged on as tightly as ever.

She went to the edge of the wood and peered across the road.

'There's a place there,' she said, 'with lots of men in. Go'n' ask them.'

William somewhat reluctantly (for his previous experiences had sadly disillusioned him with human nature in general) went through the trees to the roadside.

He looked back at the white-clad form of Goldilocks.

'Wait for me,' he whispered hoarsely.

41

Anxious to attract as little notice as possible, he crept on all fours round to the door of the public-house. He poked in his head nervously.

'Please, can some–'n—' he began politely, but in the clatter that arose the ghostly whisper was lost. Several glasses and a chair were flung at his head. Amid shoutings and uproar the innkeeper went for his gun, but on his return William had departed, and the innkeeper, who knew the better part of valour, contented himself with bolting the door and fetching sal-volatile for his wife. After a decent interval he unlocked the door and the inmates crept cautiously home one by one.

'A great, furious brute,' they were heard to say. 'Must have escaped from a circus—'

'If we hadn't been quick—'

'We ought to get up a party with guns—'

'Let's go and warn the school, or it'll get the kids—'

On reaching their homes most of them found their wives in hysterics on the kitchen floor after a hasty return from the mothers' meeting.

Meanwhile William sat beneath a tree in the wood in an attitude of utter despondency, his head on his paws.

'Why didn't you *tell* them?' said Goldilocks impatiently.

'I tell everyone,' said William. 'Nobody'll *listen* to me. They make a noise and throw things. I'm go'n' home.'

He rose and held out a paw. He felt utterly and miserably cut off from his fellow-men. He clung pathetically to Goldilocks' presence.

'Come with me,' he said.

Hand in hand, a curious couple, they went through the woods to the back of William's house. 'If I die,' he said at once, 'afore we get home, you'd better bury me. There's a spade in the back garden.'

He took her round to the shed in his back garden.

'You stay here,' he whispered. 'An' I'll try and get my head took off an' then get us somethin' to eat.'

Cautiously and apprehensively he crept into the house. He could hear his mother talking to the cook in the kitchen.

'It stood right in the window,' she was saying in a trembling voice. 'Not a very big animal but so ferocious-looking. We got out just in time – it was just getting ready to spring. It—'

William crept to the open kitchen door and assumed his most plaintive expression, forgetting for the moment that his expression could not be seen. Just as he was opening his mouth to speak, cook turned round and saw him. The scream that cook emitted sent William scampering up to his room in utter terror.

'It's gone up – plungin' into Master William's room – the *brute*! Thank evving the little darlin's out playin'. Oh, mum, the cunnin' brute's a-shut the door. Oh, my! It turned me inside out – it did. Oh, I darsn't go an' lock it in, but that's what ought to be done—'

'We – we'll get someone—' said Mrs Brown weakly. 'We – oh, here's the master.'

Mr Brown entered as she spoke. 'I've got terrible news for you,' he said.

Mrs Brown burst into tears.

'Oh, John, nothing could be worse than – than – John. Do get someone – oh, my goodness, suppose, he's there – suppose it's mangling him – *do* go—'

Mr Brown sat calmly in his chair.

'William,' he said, 'has eloped with a *jeune première* and a bear-skin. An entire Christmas pantomime is searching the village for him. They've spent the afternoon searching the wood and now they are searching the village. Father

Christmas is drinking ale in a pub. He discovered that William had paid it a visit. A Fairy Queen is sitting outside the pub complaining of toothache, and Goldilocks' mother is complimenting the vicar on the rural beauty of his village, in the intervals of weeping over the loss of her daughter. I gathered that William had visited the vicarage. There's a giant complaining of the cold, and a man in his shirt-sleeves whose language is turning the air blue for miles around. I was coming up from the station and was introduced to them as William's father. I had some difficulty in calming them, but I promised to do what I could to find the missing pair. I'm rather keen on finding William. I don't think I can do better than hand him over to them for a few minutes. As for the missing damsel—'

Mrs Brown found her voice.

'Do you mean—?' she gasped feebly, 'do you mean that it was William all the time?'

Mr Brown rose wearily.

'Of course,' he said. 'Isn't everything *always* William all the time?'

CHAPTER 3

WILLIAM'S TRUTHFUL CHRISTMAS

William went to church with his family every Sunday morning but he did not usually listen to the sermon. He considered it a waste of time. He sometimes enjoyed singing the psalms and hymns. Any stone-deaf person could have told when William was singing the psalms and hymns by the expressions of pain on the faces of those around him. William's singing was loud and discordant. It completely drowned the organ and the choir. Miss Barney, who stood just in front of him, said that it always gave her a headache for the rest of the week. William contested with some indignation that he had as good a right to sing in church as anyone. Besides, there was nothing wrong with his voice . . . It was just like everyone else's . . .

During the Vicar's sermon, William either stared at the

curate (William always scored in this game because the curate invariably began to grow pink and look embarrassed after about five minutes of William's stare) or held a face-pulling competition with the red-haired choir boy or amused himself with insects, conveyed to church in a match box in his pocket, till restrained by the united glares of his father and mother and Ethel and Robert . . .

But this Sunday, attracted by the frequent repetition of the word 'Christmas', William put his stag beetle back into its box and gave his whole attention to the Vicar's exhortation . . .

'What is it that poisons our whole social life?' said the Vicar earnestly. 'What is it that spoils even the holy season that lies before us? It is deceit. It is untruthfulness. Let each one of us decide here and now for this season of Christmas at least, to cast aside all deceit and hypocrisy and speak the truth one with another . . . It will be the first step to a holier life. It will make this Christmas the happiest of our lives . . .'

William's attention was drawn from the exhortation by the discovery that he had not quite closed the match box and the stag beetle was crawling up Ethel's coat.

Fortunately Ethel was busily engaged in taking in all the details of Marion Hatherly's new dress across the aisle and did not notice. William recaptured his pet and shut up the match box . . . then rose to join lustily and inharmoniously in the first verse of 'Onward, Christian Soldiers'. During the other verses he employed himself by trying a perfectly new grimace (which he had been practising all week) on the choir boy. It was intercepted by the curate who shuddered and looked away hastily. The sight and sound of William in the second row from the front completely spoilt the service for the curate every Sunday. He was an aesthetic young man and William's appearance and personality hurt his sense of beauty . . .

But the words of the sermon had made a deep impression on William. He decided for this holy season at least to cast aside deceit and hypocrisy and speak the truth one with another . . . William had not been entirely without aspiration to a higher life before this. He had once decided to be self-sacrificing for a whole day and his efforts had been totally unappreciated and misunderstood. He had once tried to reform others and the result had been even more disastrous. But he'd never made a real effort to cast aside deceit and hypocrisy and to speak the truth one with another. He decided to try it at Christmas as the Vicar had suggested.

Much to his disgust William heard that Uncle Frederick and Aunt Emma had asked his family to stay with them for Christmas. He gathered that the only drawback to the arrangement in the eyes of his family was himself, and the probable effect of his personality on the peaceful household of Uncle Frederick and Aunt Emma. He was not at all offended. He was quite used to this view of himself.

'All right!' he said obligingly. 'You jus' go. I don' mind. I'll stay at home . . . you jus' leave me money an' my presents an' I won't mind a bit.'

William's spirits in fact soared sky-high at the prospect of such an oasis of freedom in the desert of parental interference. But his family betrayed again that strange disinclination to leave William to his own devices that hampered so many of William's activities.

'No, William,' said his mother, 'we certainly can't do that. You'll have to come with us but I do hope you'll be good.'

William remembered the sermon and his good resolution.

'Well,' he said cryptically, 'I guess 'f you knew what I was goin' to be like at Christmas you'd almost *want* me to come.'

It happened that William's father was summoned on Christmas Eve to the sick bed of one of his aunts and so could not accompany them, but they set off under Robert's leadership and arrived safely.

Uncle Frederick and Aunt Emma were very stout and good-natured looking, but Uncle Frederick was the stouter and more good-natured-looking of the two. They had not seen William since he was a baby. That explained the fact of their having invited William and his family to spend Christmas with them. They lived too far away to have heard even rumours of the horror with which William inspired the grown-up world around him. They greeted William kindly.

'So this is little William,' said Uncle Frederick, putting his hand on William's head. 'And how is little William?'

William removed his head from Uncle Frederick's hand in silence then said distantly, 'V' well, thank you.'

'And so grateful to your Uncle and Aunt for asking you

to stay with them, aren't you, William?' went on his mother.

William remembered that his career of truthfulness did not begin till the next day so he said still more distantly, 'Yes.'

That evening Ethel said to her mother in William's presence, 'Well, he's not been so *bad* today, considering.'

'You wait,' said William unctuously. 'You wait till tomorrow when I start castin' aside deceit an' . . . an'— Today'll be *nothin'* to it.'

William awoke early on Christmas Day. He had hung up his stocking the night before and was pleased to see it fairly full. He took out the presents quickly but not very optimistically. He had been early disillusioned in the matter of grown-ups' capacity for choosing suitable presents. Memories of prayer books and history books and socks and handkerchiefs floated before his mental vision . . . Yes, as bad as ever! . . . a case containing a pen and pencil and ruler, a new brush and comb, a purse (empty) and a new tie . . . a penknife and a box of toffee were the only redeeming features. On the chair by his bedside was a book of Church History from Aunt Emma and a box containing a pair of compasses, a protractor and a set square from Uncle Frederick . . .

William dressed, but as it was too early to go down he sat down on the floor and ate all his tin of toffee. Then he turned his attention to his Church History book. He read a few pages but the character and deeds of the saintly Aidan so exasperated him that he was driven to relieve his feeling by taking his new pencil from its case and adorning the saint's picture by the addition of a top hat and spectacles. He completed the alterations by a moustache and by changing the book the saint held into an attaché case. He made similar alterations to every picture in the book . . . St Oswald seemed much improved by them and this cheered William considerably. Then he took his penknife and began to carve his initials upon his brush and comb . . .

William appeared at breakfast wearing his new tie and having brushed his hair with his new brush or rather with what was left of his new brush after his very drastic initial-carving. He carried under his arm his presents for his host and hostess. He exchanged 'Happy Christmas' gloomily.

His resolve to cast away deceit and hypocrisy and speak the truth one with another lay heavy upon him. He regarded it as an obligation that could not be shirked. William was a boy of great tenacity of purpose. Having once made up his mind to a course, he pursued it regardless of consequences . . .

'Well, William, darling,' said his mother, 'did you find your presents?'

'Yes,' said William gloomily. 'Thank you.'

'Did you like the book and instruments that Uncle and I gave you?' said Aunt Emma brightly.

'No,' said William gloomily and truthfully. 'I'm not int'rested in Church History an' I've got something like those at school. Not that I'd want 'em,' he added hastily, 'if I hadn't 'em.'

'*William!*' screamed Mrs Brown in horror. 'How can you be so ungrateful!'

'I'm not ungrateful,' explained William wearily. 'I'm only bein' truthful. I'm casting aside deceit an' . . . an' hyp—hyp—what he said. I'm only sayin' that I'm not int'rested in Church History nor in those inst'ments. But thank you very much for 'em.'

There was a gasp of dismay and a horrified silence

during which William drew his paper packages from under his arm.

'Here are your Christmas presents from me,' he said.

The atmosphere brightened. They unfastened their parcels with expressions of anticipation and Christian forgiveness upon their faces. William watched them, his face 'registering' only patient suffering.

'It's very kind of you,' said Aunt Emma still struggling with the string.

'It's not kind,' said William still treading doggedly the path of truth. 'Mother said I'd got to bring you something.'

Mrs. Brown coughed suddenly and loudly but not in time to drown the fatal words of truth . . .

'But still – er – very kind,' said Aunt Emma, though with less enthusiasm.

At last she brought out a small pincushion.

'Thank you very much, William,' she said. 'You really oughtn't to have spent your money on me like this.'

'I din't,' said William stonily. 'I hadn't any money, but I'm very glad you like it. It was left over from Mother's stall at the Sale of Work, an' Mother said it was no use keepin' it for nex' year because it had got so faded.'

Again Mrs Brown coughed loudly but too late. Aunt Emma said coldly:

'I see. Yes. Your mother was quite right. But thank you all the same, William.'

Uncle Frederick had now taken the wrappings from his present and held up a leather purse.

'Ah, this is a really useful present,' he said jovially.

'I'm 'fraid it's not very useful,' said William. 'Uncle Jim sent it to Father for his birthday but Father said it was no use 'cause the catch wouldn' catch so he gave it to me to give to you.'

Uncle Frederick tried the catch.

'Um . . . ah . . .' he said. 'Your father was quite right. The catch won't catch. Never mind, I'll send it back to your father as a New Year present . . . what?'

As soon as the Brown family were left alone it turned upon William in a combined attack.

'I *warned* you!' said Ethel to her mother.

'He ought to be punished,' said Robert.

'William, how *could* you?' said Mrs Brown.

'When I'm bad, you go on at me,' said William with exasperation, 'an' when I'm tryin' to lead a holier life and cast aside hyp— hyp— what he said, you go on at me. I dunno what I *can* be. I don't mind bein' hung. I'd as soon be punished as keep havin' Christmas over an' over again simply every year the way we do . . .'

William accompanied the party to church after breakfast. He was slightly cheered by discovering a choir boy with a natural aptitude for grimaces and an instinctive knowledge of the rules of the game. The Vicar preached an unconvincing sermon on unselfishness and the curate gave full play to an ultra-Oxford accent and a voice that was almost as unmusical as William's. Aunt Emma said it had been a 'beautiful service'. The only bright spot to William was when the organist boxed the ears of the youngest choir boy, who retaliated by putting out his tongue at the organist at the beginning of each verse of the last hymn . . .

William was very silent during lunch . . . He simply didn't know what people saw in Christmas. It was just like ten Sundays rolled into one . . . An' they didn't even give people the sort of presents they'd like . . . No one all his life had ever given him a water pistol or a catapult or a trumpet or bows and arrows or anything really useful . . . And if they didn't like truth an' castin' aside deceit an – an' the other thing, they could do without . . . but he was jolly well goin' to go on with it. He'd made up his mind and he was jolly well goin' to go on with it . . . His silence was greatly welcomed by his family. He ate plentifully, however, of the turkey and plum pudding and felt strangely depressed afterwards . . . so much that he followed the example of the rest of the family and went up to his bedroom . . .

There he brushed his hair with his new brush, but he had carved his initials so deeply and spaciously that the brush came in two with the first flourish. He brushed his shoes with the two halves with great gusto in the manner of the professional shoe polish . . . Then having nothing else to do, he turned to his Church History again. The desecrated pictures of the Saints met his gaze and realising suddenly the enormity of the crime in grown-up eyes he took his penknife and cut them all out. He made paper boats of them, and deliberately and because he hated it he cut his new tie into strips to fasten some of the boats together. He organised a thrilling naval battle with them and was almost forgetting his grudge against life in general and Christmas in particular . . .

He was roused to the sense of the present by sounds of life and movement downstairs, and, thrusting his saintly paper fleet into his pyjama case, he went down to the drawing-room. As he entered there came the sound of a car drawing up at the front door and Uncle Frederick looked out of the window and groaned aloud.

'It's Lady Atkinson,' he said. 'Help! Help!'

'Now, Frederick, dear,' said Aunt Emma hastily. 'Don't talk like that and *do* try to be nice to her. She's one of *the* Atkinsons, you know,' she explained with empressement to Mrs Brown in a whisper as the lady was shown in.

Lady Atkinson was stout and elderly and wore a very youthful hat and coat.

'A happy Christmas to you all!' she said graciously. 'The boy? Your nephew? William? How do you do, William? He – *stares* rather, doesn't he? Ah, yes,' she greeted everyone separately with infinite condescension.

'I've brought you my Christmas present in person,' she went on in the tone of voice of one giving an unheard-of treat. 'Look!'

She took out of an envelope a large signed photograph of herself. 'There now . . . what do you think of that?'

Murmurs of surprise and admiration and gratitude.

Lady Atkinson drank them in complacently.

'It's very good, isn't it? You . . . little boy . . . don't you think it's very like me?'

William gazed at it critically.

'It's not as horrid as you are,' was his final offering at the altar of truth.

'*William!*' screamed Mrs Brown. 'How *can* you be so impolite!'

'Impolite?' said William with some indignation. 'I'm not tryin' to be polite! I'm bein' truthful. I can't be everything. Seems to me I'm the only person in the world what *is* truthful an' no one seems to be grateful to me. It *isn't*'s as what she is,' he went on doggedly, 'an' it's not got as many little lines on its face as what she has an' it's different lookin' altogether. It looks pretty an' she doesn't—'

Lady Atkinson towered over him, quivering with rage.

'You *nasty* little boy!' she said thrusting her face close to his. 'You – NASTY – little – boy!'

Then she swept out of the room without another word.

The front door slammed.

She was gone.

Aunt Emma sat down and began to weep.

'She'll never come to the house again,' she said.

'I always said he ought to be punished,' said Robert gloomily. 'Every day we let him off he complicates our lives still worse.'

'I shall tell your father, William,' said Mrs Brown, '*directly* we get home.'

'The kindest thing to think,' said Ethel, 'is that he's troublesome.'

'Well,' said William, 'I don' know what I've done 'cept cast aside deceit an' – an' the other thing what he said in church an' speak the truth an' that. I don' know why everyone's so mad at me jus' 'cause of that. You'd think they'd be glad!'

'She'll never set foot in the house again,' sobbed Aunt Emma.

Uncle Frederick, who had been vainly trying to hide his glee, rose.

'I don't think she will, my dear,' he said cheerfully. 'Nothing like the truth, William . . . absolutely nothing.'

He pressed a half-crown into William's hand surreptitiously as he went to the door . . .

'DON'T YOU THINK IT'S VERY LIKE ME?' ASKED LADY
ATKINSON. 'IT'S NOT LIKE YOU ARE,' SAID WILLIAM,
CRITICALLY. 'I'M NOT IMPOLITE. I'M BEING TRUTHFUL.'

*

A diversion was mercifully caused at this moment by the arrival of the post. Among it there was a Christmas card from an artist who had a studio about five minutes' walk from the house. This little attention comforted Aunt Emma very much.

'How kind of him!' she said, 'and we never sent him anything. But there's that calendar that Mr Franks sent to us and it's not written on. Perhaps William could be trusted to take it to Mr Fairly with our compliments while the rest of us go for a short walk.' She looked at William rather coldly.

William, who was feeling the atmosphere indoors inexplicably hostile (except for Uncle Frederick's equally inexplicable friendliness), was glad of an excuse for escaping.

He set off with the calendar wrapped in brown paper. On the way his outlook on life was considerably brightened by finding a street urchins' fight in full swing. He joined in it with gusto and was soon acclaimed leader of his side. This exhilarating adventure was ended by a policeman, who scattered the combatants and pretended to chase William down a side street in order to vary the monotony of his Christmas 'beat'.

William, looking rather battered and dishevelled, arrived at Mr Fairly's studio. The calendar had fortunately survived the battle unscathed and William handed it to Mr Fairly who opened the door. Mr Fairly showed him into the studio with a low bow. Mr Fairly was clothed in correct artistic style . . . baggy trousers, velvet coat and a flowing tie. He had a pointed beard and a theatrical manner. He had obviously lunched well – as far as liquid refreshment was concerned at any rate. He was moved to tears by the calendar.

'How kind! How very kind . . . My dear young friend, forgive this emotion. The world is hard. I am not used to kindness. It unmans me . . .'

He wiped away his tears with a large mauve and yellow handkerchief. William gazed at it fascinated.

'If you will excuse me, my dear young friend,' went on Mr Fairly, 'I will retire to my bedroom where I have the wherewithal to write and indite a letter of thanks to your most delightful and charming relative. I beg you to make yourself at home here . . . Use my house, my dear young friend, as though it were your own . . .'

He waved his arms and retreated unsteadily to an inner room, closing the door behind him.

William sat down on a chair and waited. Time passed, William became bored. Suddenly a fresh aspect of his Christmas resolution occurred to him. If you were speaking the truth one with another yourself, surely you might take everything that other people said for truth . . . He'd said, 'Use this house, my dear young friend, as though it were your own . . .' Well, he would. The man prob'ly meant it . . . well, anyway, he shouldn't have said it if he didn't . . . William went across the room and opened a cupboard. It contained a medley of paints, two palettes, two oranges and a cake. The feeling of oppression that had followed William's Christmas lunch had faded and he attacked the cake with gusto. It took about ten minutes to finish the cake and about four to finish the oranges. William felt refreshed. He looked round the studio with renewed interest. A lay figure sat upon a couch on a small platform. William approached it cautiously. It was almost life-size and clad in a piece of thin silk. William lifted it. It was quite light. He put it on a chair by the window. Then he went to the little back room. A bonnet and mackintosh (belonging to Mr Fairly's charwoman) hung there. He dressed the lay figure in the bonnet and mackintosh. He found a piece of black gauze in a drawer and put it over the figure's face as a veil and tied it round the bonnet. He felt all the thrill of the creative artist. He shook hands with it and talked to it. He began to have a feeling of deep affection for it. He called it Annabel. The clock struck and he remembered the note he was waiting for . . . He knocked gently at the bedroom door. There was no answer. He opened the door and entered. On the writing-table by the door was a letter:

'DEAR FRIEND,
'Many thanks for your beautiful calendar. Words fail me . . .'

Then came a blot – mingled ink and emotion – and that was all. Words had failed Mr Fairly so completely that he lay outstretched on the sofa by the window sleeping the sleep of the slightly inebriated. William thought he'd better not wake him up. He returned to the studio and carried on his self-imposed task of investigation. He found some acid drops in a drawer adhering to a tube of yellow ochre. He separated them and ate the acid drops but their strong flavour of yellow ochre made him feel sick and he returned to Annabel for sympathy . . .

Then he thought of a game. The lay figure was a captured princess and William was the gallant rescuer. He went outside, opened the front door cautiously, crept into the hall, hid behind the door, dashed into the studio, caught up the figure in his arms and dashed into the street with it. The danger and exhilaration of a race for freedom through the streets with Annabel in his arms was too enticing to be resisted. As a matter of fact the flight through the streets was rather disappointing. He met no one and no one pursued him . . .

He staggered up the steps to Aunt Emma's house still carrying Annabel. There, considering the matter for the first time in cold blood, he realised that his rescue of Annabel was not likely to be received enthusiastically by his home circle. And Annabel was not easy to conceal. The house seemed empty but he could already hear its inmates returning from their walk. He felt a sudden hatred of Annabel for being so large and unhideable. He could not reach the top of the stairs before they came in at the door. The drawing-room door was open and into it he rushed, deposited Annabel in a chair by the fireplace with her back to the room, and returned to the hall. He smoothed back his hair, assumed his most vacant expression and awaited them. To his surprise they crept past the drawing-room door on tiptoe and congregated in the dining-room.

'A caller,' said Aunt Emma. 'Did you see?'

'Yes, in the dining-room,' said Mrs Brown. 'I saw her hat through the window.'

'Curse!' said Uncle Frederick.

'The maids must have shown her in before they went up to change. I'm simply *not* going to see her. On Christmas Day, too! I'll just wait till she gets tired and goes or till one of the maids comes down and can send her away!'

'Sh!' said Uncle Frederick. 'She'll hear you.'

Aunt Emma lowered her voice.

'I don't think she's a lady,' she said. 'She didn't look it through the window.'

'Perhaps she's collecting for something,' said Mrs Brown.

'Well,' said Aunt Emma sinking her voice to a

conspiratorial whisper. 'If we stay in here and keep very quiet she'll get tired of waiting and go.'

William was torn between an interested desire to be safely out of the way when the dénouement took place and a disinterested desire to witness the dénouement. The latter won and he stood at the back of the group with a sphinx-like expression upon his freckled face . . .

They waited in silence for some minutes then Aunt Emma said, 'Well, she'll stay for ever it seems to me if someone doesn't send her away. Frederick, go and turn her out.'

They all crept into the hall. Uncle Frederick went just inside and coughed loudly. Annabel did not move. Uncle Frederick came back.

'Deaf!' he whispered. 'Stone deaf! Someone else try.'

Ethel advanced boldly into the middle of the room. 'Good afternoon,' she said clearly and sweetly.

Annabel did not move. Ethel returned.

'I think she must be asleep,' said Ethel.

'She looks drunk to me,' said Aunt Emma, peeping round the door.

'I shouldn't wonder if she was dead,' said Robert. 'It's

just the sort of thing you read about in books. Mysterious dead body found in drawing-room. I bet I can find a few clues to the murder if she is dead.'

'*Robert!*' reproved Mrs Brown in a shrill whisper.

'Perhaps you'd better fetch the police, Frederick,' said Aunt Emma.

ANNABEL DID NOT MOVE

'I'll have one more try,' said Uncle Frederick.

He entered the room.

'Good afternoon,' he bellowed.

Annabel did not move. He went up to her.

'Now look here, my woman—' he began, laying his hand on her shoulder . . .

'I'LL HAVE ONE MORE TRY,' SAID UNCLE FREDERICK, AND ENTERED THE ROOM. 'GOOD AFTERNOON,' HE BELLOWED.

Then the dénouement happened.

Mr Fairly burst into the house like a whirlwind still slightly inebriated and screaming with rage.

'Where's the thief? Where is he? He's stolen my figure. He's eaten my tea. I shall have to eat my supper for my tea and my breakfast for my supper . . . I shall be a meal wrong always . . . I shall never get right. And it's all his fault. Where is he? He's stolen my charwoman's clothes. He's stolen my figure. He's eaten my tea. Wait till I get him!' He caught sight of Annabel, rushed into the drawing-room, caught her up in his arms and turned round upon the circle of open-mouthed spectators. 'I *hate* you!' he screamed, 'and your nasty little calendars and your nasty little boys! Stealing my figure and eating my tea . . . I'll light the fire with your nasty little calendar. I'd like to light the fire with your nasty little boy!'

With a final snort of fury he turned, still clasping Annabel in his arms, and staggered down the front steps. Weakly, stricken and (for the moment) speechless, they watched his departure from the top of the steps. He took to his heels as soon as he was in the road. But he was less fortunate than William. As he turned the corner and vanished from sight, already two policemen were in pursuit. He was screaming defiance at them as he ran. Annabel's head wobbled over his shoulder and her bonnet dangled by a string.

Then, no longer speechless, they turned on William.

'I *told* you,' said Robert to them when there was a slight lull in the storm. 'You wouldn't take any advice. If it wasn't Christmas Day I'd . . .'

'But you won't let me *speak*!' said William plaintively. 'Jus' listen to me a minute. When I got to his house he said, he said mos' distinct, he said, "Please use this—"'

'William,' interrupted Mrs Brown with dignity. 'I don't know what's happened and I don't *want* to know but I shall tell your father *all* about it *directly* we get home.'

Uncle Frederick saw them off at the station the next day.

'Does your effort at truth continue today as well?' he said to William.

'I s'pose it's Boxing Day too,' said William. 'He din' mention Boxing Day. But I s'pose it counts with Christmas.'

'I won't ask you whether you've enjoyed yourself then,' said Uncle Frederick. He slipped another half-crown into William's hand. 'Buy yourself something with that. Your

Aunt chose the Church History book and the instruments. I'm really grateful to you about— Well, I think Emma's right. I don't think she'll ever come again.'

The train steamed out. Uncle Frederick returned home. He had been too optimistic. Lady Atkinson was in the drawing-room talking to his wife.

'Of course,' she was saying, 'I'm not annoyed. I bear no grudge because I believe the boy's *possessed*! He ought to be ex— exercised . . . You know, what you do with evil spirits.'

*

It was the evening of William's return home. His father's question as to whether William had been good had been answered as usual in the negative and, refusing to listen to details of accusation or defence (ignoring William's 'But he *said* mos' distinct, he said, "Please use this—"' and the rest of the explanation always drowned by the others), he docked William of a month's pocket money But William was not depressed. The ordeal of Christmas was over. Normal life stretched before him once more. His spirits rose. He wandered out into the lane. There he met Ginger, his bosom pal, with whom on normal days he fought and wrestled and carried out deeds of daring and wickedness, but who (like William) on festivals and holy days was forced reluctantly to shed the light of his presence upon his own family. From Ginger's face, too, a certain gloom cleared as he saw William.

'Well,' said William, ''v you enjoyed it?'

'I had a pair of braces from my aunt,' said Ginger bitterly. 'A pair of *braces*!'

'Well, I had a tie an' a Church History book.'

'I put my braces down the well.'

'I chopped up my tie into little bits.'

'Was it nice at your aunt's?'

William's grievances burst out.

'I went to church an' took what that man said an' I've been speaking the truth one with another an' leadin' a higher life an' well, it jolly well din't make it the happiest Christmas of my life what he said it would . . . It made it the worst. Everyone mad at me all the time. I think I was the only person in the world speakin' the truth one with another an' they've took off my pocket money for it. An' you'd think 'f you was speakin' the truth yourself you might take what anyone else said for truth an' I keep tellin' 'em that he said mos' distinct, "Please use this house as if it were your own", but they won' listen to me! Well, I've done with it. I'm goin' back to deceit an' – an' – what's a word beginnin' with hyp—?'

'Hypnotism?' suggested Ginger after deep thought.

'Yes, that's it,' said William. 'Well, I'm goin' back to it first thing tomorrow mornin'.'

CHAPTER 4

WILLIAM STARTS THE HOLIDAYS

The Christmas holidays had arrived and William and the other Outlaws whooped their way home from school at the unusual hour of 11 a.m., to the unaffected dismay of their families. They had listened to a stirring address from their form master (who felt as little regret at parting from the Outlaws as the Outlaws felt at parting from him), but they had been more intent upon the unauthorised distribution and mastication of a bag of nuts they had bought on the way to school than upon the high ideals which their form master was holding up for them, and so missed many words of counsel and inspiration which might (or might not) have made a difference to their whole lives.

Anyway, having finished the nuts (and deposited the shells in the satchel of their enemy, Hubert Lane), the

Outlaws leapt out of the school buildings and whooped and scuffled and shouted their way home.

'We've broke up!' yelled William, as he entered the hall, and flung his satchel with a clatter upon the floor.

Mrs Brown came out of the morning-room, rather pale at this invasion of her usual morning quiet.

'I – I'd forgotten you were breaking up today, William,' she said. Her tone betrayed no ecstatic joy at the realisation of the fact.

William turned a somersault, and came into violent collision with a small table which held a vase of flowers.

'Sorry,' said William, still cheerfully, as he repaired the damage as best he could. (That is to say, he picked up the table, replaced the vase on it, picked up the flowers, put them in the vase – mostly wrong way up – and rubbed the spilt water into the carpet with his foot.)

'Oh, don't, William!' moaned his mother. 'I'll ring for Emma – your boots are so dirty.'

'Sorry,' said William again, slightly hurt, 'I was only tryin' to help.'

'Haven't – haven't you come home rather early?' said Mrs Brown.

'No,' said William heartily, 'we always come out this time breaking-up mornings. We've broke up.' He chanted on a note that made Mrs Brown draw her brows together, and raise her hands to her ears.

'William *darling*,' she said plaintively. Then, 'What are you going to do, dear – just till lunch-time, I mean?'

There was a note of resigned hopelessness in her voice. Mrs Brown was a woman without any political ambition whatever, but if Mrs Brown had been put in charge of the Education Department of the Government for a month, she would have made several drastic changes without any hesitation. She would have made a law that no holidays should last longer than a week, and if they did, free treatment for nervous breakdown was to be provided for all mothers of families, and that on 'break-up days' school should continue until late in the evening. Mrs Brown considered it adding insult to injury to send children home at eleven o'clock in the morning on the last day of term.

'Er – what are you going to do till lunch, dear?' said Mrs Brown again.

William considered the possibilities of the universe.

'I might go into the garden an' practise with my bow and

arrow,' he said.

'Oh, *no*, dear,' said Mrs Brown, closing her eyes, 'please don't do that! It does annoy your father so when the windows get broken.'

'*Oh!*' said William indignantly. 'I keep explainin' about that. I wasn't aimin' at that window. It was just that my hand slipped jus' when I was shootin' it off. I was aimin' at somethin' quite diff'rent.'

'Yes, dear,' said Mrs Brown, 'but your hand might slip again.'

'No, I don't think it will,' said William hopefully. 'I'll try an' keep it steady – and it doesn't always break windows, you know, even when it slips.'

'No,' said Mrs Brown. '*Not* the bow and arrows, William,' and added with consummate tact, 'You don't want to risk breaking things so near Christmas, you know, William.'

There was certainly some sense in that. It was an argument that appealed to William.

'Well,' he said thoughtfully, 'there's the airgun. It's quite different from the bow and arrows,' he put in hastily. 'I think p'raps I oughter keep on practisin' with the airgun, in case there's another war.'

'No, William,' said Mrs Brown. '*Not* the airgun.' Then tentatively and without much hope, 'You – you wouldn't like to do a little quiet school work, would you, William dear, so as to keep your hand in for next term?'

'No, thank you,' said William quite firmly.

'I think it would be rather a good idea,' said Mrs Brown, still clinging to the vision of peace that the proposal summoned up to her eyes.

William considered for a moment in gloomy silence the vision of unadulterated boredom that the proposal summoned up to his eyes. Then he brightened.

'I don't think so, mother,' he said at last. 'I don't think it fair on the other boys to go workin' in the holidays.'

While Mrs Brown was slowly recovering from this startling vision of William conscientiously refraining from holiday work for the sake of his class-mates, William had yet another idea.

'S'pose I try to mend that clock that's gone wrong – the one in the dining-room,' he said brightly.

Mrs Brown groaned again. William had hoped that she'd forgotten the last occasion he'd tried to mend a clock, but she hadn't.

William had certainly succeeded in reducing it into its component parts, but having done that had not been able to resist the temptation of trying to make a motor boat of the component parts, and when finally they were taken to the clock-maker, it was discovered that three or four important component parts were missing.

William suspected a duck who had been on the pond when William had launched his motor boat and the pond had taken the motor boat to its bosom. William insisted that he had salvaged all the parts that the muddy bosom of the pond could be induced to yield, and that if there were any missing that duck must have eaten them.

William watched the duck with morbid interest for some days and imagined several times that it looked pale and unhappy. Anyway, the upshot of it all was that William's father had to buy a new clock, and that William went without pocket-money for several months. But all this had been more than a year ago. William wished that the memories of grown-ups were not so inordinately long. He'd have liked to try his hand at a clock again.

'No, William,' said Mrs Brown, 'most certainly not.'

'Well, what shall I do?' said William, slightly aggrieved.

Mrs Brown had an idea.

'Well, William, it's so near Christmas time – wouldn't you like to be thinking out some little presents for people?'

'I've hardly any money,' said William, and added enigmatically, 'what with windows and things.'

'Well,' said Mrs Brown encouragingly, 'it isn't the money you spend on them that people value. It's the thought behind it. I'm sure that with a little thought you could make some very nice presents for your relations and friends.'

William considered the idea in silence for some minutes. Then he brightened. It seemed to appeal to him.

'All right,' he said. 'I'll go an' think upstairs, shall I?'

Mrs Brown drew a breath of relief.

'Yes, William,' she said, 'I think that will be very nice.'

The plan seemed to succeed beyond Mrs Brown's fondest dreams. She did not see or hear of William for the rest of the morning. It was almost as if he were still at school. He appeared at lunch, but was silent and thoughtful. A sense of peace stole over Mrs Brown.

After lunch, Ethel and Robert came to her in the morning-room.

'I say,' said Robert in a mystified voice, 'I thought William was breaking up today.'

'He is,' said Mrs Brown. 'He has broken up. He came home about eleven o'clock.'

'He's very quiet,' said Ethel lugubriously.

Mrs Brown smiled a fond, maternal smile. 'Dear little boy,' she said. 'He's upstairs thinking out his Christmas presents to people.'

'Well,' said Robert, 'let's make the most of it, and talk over the party.'

Robert and Ethel were giving a party to their friends, and William was being let into it as little as possible. Mingled with an elder brother and sister's instinctive feeling that the admission of a small schoolboy brother into their plans would in some way cheapen the whole thing was an equally instinctive fear of William. Pies in which William had a finger had a curious way of turning into something quite unexpected. William could generally prove that it had nothing to do with him, but still – the result was the same.

So Robert's and Ethel's party was a 'secret', only to be discussed when William was safely out of the way. William, of course, knew that it was to take place and professed an utter indifference to it, while privately he spent a good deal of time and ingenuity trying to ferret out the details of it. So far they had managed to keep secret from him the fact that after supper there was going to be a short one-act play.

Ethel and Robert had lately joined the Dramatic Society and at present no function of any kind was complete to them without a one-act play. The shining lights of the Dramatic Society (including Ethel and Robert) were going to take part in the play. They kept this part of it particularly a secret from William, because William rather fancied himself both as actor and playwright, and they felt that if William knew that a play was going to take place under his roof it would be practically impossible to protect the play from the devastating effects of William's interest in it.

They discussed the dancing (which was to take place before supper) and the supper, and the play (which was to take place after supper), and Ethel's dress and Mrs Brown's dress, and the invitation list and the extra 'help' they would need for the evening, and whether Robert's dress-suit had better go to the tailors to be pressed or not.

Finally Mrs Brown became a little anxious and said to Ethel: 'Ethel, dear, I wish you'd just run upstairs and have a look at William. He's so quiet. I hope he's not feeling ill or anything.'

Visible gloom settled on the faces of Robert and Ethel at the mention of William.

'Ill!' repeated Robert with deep feeling.

'Yes, you know, mother,' said Ethel, 'we'd hear enough row if he felt ill. But—'

She went obediently from the room and Mrs Brown and Robert continued the discussion. Just as they were deciding that Robert's suit had better go to be pressed they were interrupted by a cry of 'Mother!' from Ethel upstairs, and leapt to their feet: 'Oh, it's William,' moaned Mrs Brown; 'he *is* ill.'

'More likely he's set the house on fire,' said Robert gloomily.

They dashed upstairs. William, his face and hands and hair and clothes freely adorned with green paint, sat on his bedroom hearthrug, which had shared in the wholesale application of green paint. On the hearthrug was a once-white straw hat of Ethel's, upon which William had obviously devoted much labour and green paint. He had, moreover, filled it with earth, and planted in it a cyclamen from the greenhouse.

'Look,' said Ethel, almost – but not quite – speechless with fury. 'My – my best hat!'

'Why, it's quite an ole hat, Ethel,' said William. 'I've seen you wear it heaps. I thought you must have about done with it.'

'LOOK!' CRIED ETHEL, ALMOST SPEECHLESS WITH FURY. 'MY – MY BEST HAT!'

'B-but, William,' gasped Mrs Brown, 'what on earth have you been doing?'

'Well, you said *think* out Christmas presents, an' *make* 'em an' don' spend money on 'em, so I thought I'd start on Ethel's, an' it took me ever so long to think of anything that I could make and that wouldn't cost money an' then I thought that I could paint one of Ethel's hats an' make it look like a kind of fancy plant pot with the paint from the shed, an' put a plant into it from the greenhouse. I thought it was rather a good idea,' he ended modestly.

'But my *hat*!' almost sobbed Ethel.

'It's a straw hat,' urged William. 'You don't want a *straw* hat in the winter.'

'But it was almost new. I want it for next summer.'

'Oh, next summer,' said William patiently. 'I guess this flower won't last as long as that. I guess you can use it again next summer.'

'And have you taken any of my things?' demanded Robert sternly.

'No, Robert,' said William meekly. 'I haven't, honestly. I was just *thinking* how I could make a nice cushion for mother out of two of your coloured handkerchiefs, stuffed with some ole things of mine, but I hadn't taken 'em, not yet.'

That was why, when William discovered about the play, he was told that he was not to see it either at rehearsals or on the evening of the party.

'Well,' said William, 'if you messed up one of my ole caps, d'you think I'd make that fuss? Not that I *mind* not seeing the ole play,' he added hastily. 'In fact,' putting himself well out of Robert's reach, 'it's rather a relief to me. I'm jolly sorry for the poor folks that have gotter watch poor Ethel and Robert tryin' to act.'

Then he leapt lightly over the window sill into the garden before Robert could get at him.

The day of the party arrived. William, shining with cleanliness, his hair brushed and greased to a resplendent sleekness, encased in his Eton suit, an expression of frowning intensity upon his freckled face, stood a little way from the rest of his family as the guests began to arrive. Some of the guests called out: 'Hello, William.' Others ignored him.

William tried to look bored and indifferent, and as if he didn't think much of the whole show. But really he was looking forward to the dancing and the supper, and he meant to watch the play from the garden through the window, even if he were not officially allowed among the audience. Absurd to let a perfectly good weapon against Robert and Ethel, that would probably do service for months and months, escape him like that.

The guests had all arrived. The music for the dancing had begun. William stood in the drawing-room, which had been 'turned out' for the dance and looked around him critically.

He slowly eliminated from his list of possible partners a girl with red hair, another with a too long neck, another with the wrong shaped nose, and another with a slight cast in her eye.

Slowly, by a process of elimination, he determined on the prettiest girl in the room, and walked across to her, baring his teeth in what was meant to be an ingratiating smile. Just as he was a few yards from her, Robert came up and claimed her, and they both moved off without looking at him. William's smile died away. He looked round the room again.

Well, that girl wasn't bad – the one with curly hair and the yellow dress. William assumed the smile again and walked

WELL, THE GIRL WASN'T TOO BAD, WILLIAM DECIDED –
THE ONE WITH CURLY HAIR AND THE YELLOW DRESS.

**WILLIAM ASSUMED HIS SMILE AGAIN AND
WALKED ACROSS TO HER.**

across to her. Just as he was approaching her a friend of Robert's came up, put his arm round her waist, and off they went together. William took off the smile. His face wore an expression of sardonic bitterness. All the girls seemed to be dancing now. No, there was the one with the wrong shaped nose still sitting by the window. William glared at her critically across the room. She wasn't so bad, really, if you didn't look at her sideways. William summoned up his painful grin and went across to her.

'May I—?' he began with excessive politeness.

A large man stepped in front of him, took the girl's hand, and led her off among the dancers.

William was boiling with fury. A nice set of people Robert and Ethel had invited. They didn't seem to know how to *behave*. There was only the girl with the squint left. William looked at her for a long time with an intent frown. She wasn't really so bad, especially when she was looking at the ground. William bared his teeth again (his jaws were aching by this time) and walked up to her.

'Excuse me—' he began.

A man stepped up from the other side.

'Shall us?' he said to the girl, and off they went.

William stood, his hands in his pockets, leaning against the wall, a ferocious frown upon his polished face. Everyone was dancing now, except a few couples who were sitting in the alcove talking and laughing. Nice lot of *manners* they'd got, thought William bitterly. Simply no one taking the slightest notice of him.

Not that he *cared*, of course, but you'd have thought that *someone* would've wanted to dance with him. Nice thing when you wasted every Wednesday afternoon at a beastly dancing lesson, and then when you went to a dance no one wanted to dance with you. Nice thing going to all this trouble of washing and hair-brushing, and putting on your best suit, just to watch other people dancing. Huh!

William turned and went with scornful dignity from the room. The only thing that in his eyes spoilt the effect of his scornful exit was a definite and very well-founded suspicion that no one had noticed it.

He went to the side door, and looked out into the night. Ginger, Douglas and Henry were coming cautiously up the walk. Now, the Outlaws, though never encouraged socially by each other's families, yet took a great interest in the social activities of each other's families.

Whenever any of them gave a party the Outlaws would be there – uninvited and very unofficial guests – generally in the garden keeping a friendly eye on the affair through the windows. William was glad that his friends had only just arrived and had not witnessed his ignominious failure to secure a partner a few minutes ago. To his friends William exaggerated his own importance at his family's festivities.

'Hello!' whispered the Outlaws. 'How're you getting on?'

'Fine,' said William, with rather overdone enthusiasm.

'We thought p'raps you'd be dancing,' said Ginger.

'Oh, I got a bit tired of dancing,' said William airily, 'an' came out to get cool. Come round an' have a look at 'em.'

Glad to be with his friends once more, he led the Outlaws round to a part of the garden where they could see the drawing-room, and, hidden among the bushes, watched the festive scene within.

'Quite a lot of 'em,' said Ginger, impressed.

'Oh, yes,' said William, 'an' there's really a lot more than there looks.'

'Has Ethel got a new dress for it?' said Douglas.

'Oh, yes,' said William. 'Everyone's got new clothes for

it. I'd better go in again soon. They don't want me to be away long.'

'Which one was you dancin' with?' said Henry.

William gave a short laugh.

'Goodness! I can't remember all the ones I was dancing with!' he said.

'Is there a good supper?' said Ginger.

'There just *is*!' said William. 'Come and look at it.'

They crept through the side door and into the dining-room. There William proudly pointed to the table, resplendent with ices and creams and fruit and trifles and jellies of every kind. The Outlaws licked their lips.

'*Crumbs!*' gasped Ginger. 'Doesn't it make you feel empty.'

'You can have a go at it when they've finished,' promised William generously. 'I'll tell you when they've all gone back. They're going to do a play afterwards.'

'*Crumbs!*' said Ginger again. 'Is it a good one?'

'I should just *think* so,' said William enthusiastically.

'Can we watch through the window?' said Henry.

'Cert'n'ly,' said William kindly, 'an' I'll come out and watch it with you. I don't suppose they'll notice I'm not sittin' with them in the room.'

'P'raps we'd better be goin' now,' said Henry, ''case they come. The music's stopped an' they're kind of movin' about.'

But it was too late. There came the sound of the opening of the drawing-room door, and an influx of guests into the hall.

'Get under the table, quick!' said William.

So the Outlaws got under the table – quick.

The guests entered. They found William apparently alone, an expression of mingled innocence and boredom and long enduring patience upon his frowning freckled face. He was engaged in arranging the chairs round the table.

'Here's the ubiquitous William,' said one of Robert's friends. William hoped that the look he received in return made him feel small. Ubiquitous, indeed. When he'd washed his face, and brushed his hair, and put on his best suit, and looked as smart as any of them.

They sat round the table. William was right at the corner, next to a tall, pale man who was suspected of cherishing a romantic passion for Ethel. The food was in the centre of the table, so the tall, pale man had to hand the dishes to

William and keep him supplied. He tried at first to talk to William, but found this difficult.

'I suppose you've broken up?' he said.

'Yes,' said William, his voice and face equally devoid of expression.

'Do you like the holidays?'

'Yes,' said William in the same tone of voice.

'Are you fond of lessons?'

'No.'

'I expect you're looking forward to Christmas.'

William, considering this remark beneath contempt, vouchsafed no answer. The tall, thin man, crushed, transferred his attention to the lady on the other side of him.

Now William was painfully conscious of the presence of Ginger and Henry and Douglas beneath the table. He realised, too, that he had towards them the duties of a host. He could not eat in comfort with Ginger, Douglas and Henry cramped and uncomfortable and hungry in his so immediate vicinity. He took two bites at the sausage roll with which the tall, thin man had supplied him, then, looking dreamily at the opposite wall, slipped his hand under the table.

There another hand, grateful and unseen, promptly relieved him of the rest of the sausage roll. His plate was empty. The tall, thin man looked at it. Then he looked at William. William met his eyes with an aggressive stare.

The tall, thin man looked at William's plate again. It was true. This child really had consumed a large sausage roll in less than a minute. He handed him the plate of sausage rolls again.

Again William took one.

Again William took two small bites and handed the rest to his invisible friends beneath the table.

Again he turned his aggressive stare upon the tall, thin man.

Again the young man looked with rising horror from William to the empty plate in front of him, and then from the empty plate back to William.

He then took the whole dish of sausage rolls, put them just in front of William, and turned to continue his conversation with his other neighbour. William felt cheered. This was just what he wanted. He took a roll on to his plate and looked round. No one was watching him. With a lightning movement he transferred the roll to his knee and held it out beneath the table. The unseen recipient grabbed it eagerly. William did the same with a second, a third, a fourth. He grew reckless. He put down a fifth, a sixth, a seventh. That was two each. He was doing them jolly well. There were three more on the dish. He'd give them those, too, and then he'd begin to eat something himself. One – two – three—

He twitched them all quickly from the dish to his plate, from his plate to the unseen hand. No more were within his reach. He turned his aggressive stare upon the tall, thin man. As though hypnotised by the stare, the tall, thin man turned slowly to William. He looked at the empty plate and the empty dish in front of William and his jaw dropped open weakly.

He put his hand to his head, and pinched himself to make sure he was awake. He simply couldn't believe his eyes. It was like a dreadful nightmare. In a few seconds this child had eaten up a large dishful of enormous sausage rolls – he must be suffering from some horrible disease. William did not speak, merely fixed him with that hungry, unflinching stare. The tall, thin man tried to say, 'And what can I pass you now?' but he couldn't. Words wouldn't come. The sight of that enormous empty dish had broken his nerve.

Just then a diversion occurred. A friend of Ethel's almost opposite had slipped off her shoe under the table, and a few minutes later reached out for it, and could not find it. She made a large circular sweep in search of it with her stockinged foot and just caught Ginger on the neck above his collar where he was most ticklish. Ginger dropped his half-eaten sausage roll and gave a loud yell. A sudden tense silence fell over the table. Had the proverbial pin been dropped, it would have been heard for miles. Then the girl who had tickled Ginger gave an embarrassed little giggle.

'I'm afraid I kicked your dog – or your cat – or something,' she said. She lifted up the table-cloth and grew pale. 'It's boys,' she said in a breathless whisper; 'ever so many of them!'

It was half an hour later. Ginger, Douglas and Henry had been ignominiously ejected. William had been dispatched to spend the rest of the evening in his bedroom. The dining-room was empty. Only three pathetic half-eaten sausage rolls beneath the table were left to tell the tale.

William leant out of his bedroom window. The shadowy forms of the Outlaws lurked in the bushes beneath.

'What're they doin' now?' whispered William.

'They're acting the play,' whispered Douglas, 'an' everyone is watching – maids an' all.'

'Well, go an' watch it,' whispered William, 'an' tell me about it tomorrow. Tell me about Robert an' Ethel – speshly if they do anythin' silly—An', I say—'

'Yes?' whispered the faithful Outlaws from the bushes.

'I'm awful hungry. I only had a few bites of roll – go an' see if there's anyone in the dining-room and if the stuff's still there.'

'There won't be anyone in the dining-room,' whispered Henry, ''cause everyone's in watching the play.'

'Well, go an' get a lot of grub,' ordered William in a sibilant commanding whisper. 'Keep some for yourself an' put some in a basket, an' I'll throw down a rope to draw it up.'

This method of obtaining food appealed greatly to William's romance-loving soul.

The Outlaws departed and in a few minutes returned – very quickly.

'William,' said Ginger excitedly, 'there's a burglar in the dinin'-room.'

'What!' said William.

'A burglar with his bag of tools an' his bag of booty, an' everything. He's drinkin' wine or somethin' at the sideboard.'

In less than a minute William had joined the Outlaws in the garden, and together they all went round to the dining-room window. Yes, there he was – a real burglar in dingy clothes and shabby necktie, a cap pulled low over his eyes, his bag of tools and a half-filled sack by him. He was standing at the sideboard drinking a whisky and soda.

The Outlaws retired to the bushes to discuss their tactics.

'We'd better go'n tell your father,' said Douglas.

'No, we *won't*,' said William, 'we'll catch him ourselves. What's the fun of findin' a burglar an' lettin' someone else catch him?'

Henry and Ginger agreed with him. William assumed the position of leader. There was an enormous curtain in a box upstairs. They'd used it for theatricals once. Robert and Ethel had got a new one for this year, but the old one would do nicely to catch the burglar in. It hadn't many holes.

'What'll we do with him, then?' said Ginger.

'We'll – we'll lock him up somewhere,' said William, as he went up to fetch the curtain.

In less than a minute he returned with it. It was certainly voluminous enough. The Outlaws laid their plans. They crept into the dining-room silently and, stealing up behind him, enveloped their prey, just as he was in the act of pouring out some more whisky. He was taken completely by surprise. He lost his footing and fell forward into a dusky mass of all-enveloping green serge. He was not a big man or a strong man. He tried to regain his footing and failed. In his green serge covering he was being dragged somewhere. He shouted.

It happened that in the morning-room (where the play was being held) Ethel, in her capacity of heroine, had just finished singing a song, which was greeted with frenzied applause by her loyal guests. The applause drowned the burglar's shouts. Douglas flung open the French windows that led from the dining-room to the garden, and panting, tugging and perspiring the Outlaws dragged their victim out into the night across the lawn. Douglas opened the greenhouse door. They hoisted the large green curtain, which still contained its struggling inhabitant, into the greenhouse, shut the door and turned the key in the lock. Then, still panting and purple-faced, the Outlaws went back to the house.

'Well, he *was* a weight!' commented Douglas.

'Shall we go an' tell 'em now?' said Ginger.

But William was still rent by the pangs of hunger.

'Oh, he's all right for a bit,' he said. 'He can't get out. Let's take a bit of food upstairs first. We can tell 'em after.'

The Outlaws approved of this. It was certainly a wise plan to make sure of the food. They returned to the dining-room, heaped several plates with dainties that particularly appealed to them, and crept silently upstairs to William's bedroom. There they sat on the floor munching happily and discussing their capture. They were just deciding that it would be rather fun to be policemen when they grew up, when Ginger pricked up his ears.

'Seems a sort of noise going on downstairs,' he said.

Very softly the Outlaws opened the door of William's bedroom and crept on to the landing. There was most certainly a sort of noise going on downstairs. Everyone seemed to be bustling about, and talking excitedly.

'Do be quiet a minute while I ring up his mother,' said

Ethel's voice, distraught and tearful. 'Hello – hello – Is that Mrs Langley? *Has* Harold come home? *Hasn't* he? – No, he's completely disappeared – No one knows *where* he is – we got to the point in the play where he comes on – just after my song, you know – and I waited and *waited* and he never came, and I had to leave the stage without finishing the scene. My nerves had absolutely all gone. I'm still trembling all over, and everyone was hunting and *hunting* for him – and we had to stop the play,' tearfully; 'we couldn't go on without him. He was the burglar, you know – I do hope nothing awful's happened – I mean, I hope he didn't get so nervous he lost his memory, or – or – went out and had some awful accident or anything. We're all do distressed – it's quite spoilt the party, of course, and *ruined* the play. We only got to the song – I don't know when I've felt so awful.'

She was interrupted by Mrs Brown's voice, high and hysterical. 'Oh, Ethel, do fetch your father. It's too dark to see anything – but there's the most awful commotion going on in the garden. Someone's breaking all the glass in the greenhouse.'

The entire party sallied out excitedly into the garden.

They were not there long, but during their absence two things happened. The Outlaws, acting with great presence of mind, seized their share of the food and fled like so many flashes of streaked lightning to their several homes. And William got into bed and went to sleep. He went to sleep with almost incredible rapidity. When his family entered his bedroom a few minutes later, demanding explanation, William lay red and breathless, but determinedly and unwakably asleep. The grimly set lines of his mouth and the frown on his brow testified to the intense and concentrated nature of his sleep.

'Oh, don't wake him,' pleaded Mrs Brown. 'It's so bad for children to be *startled* out of sleep.'

'Sleep!' said Robert sarcastically. 'Well, I don't mind. It can wait till tomorrow for all I care. The party's *ruined*, anyway.'

Fortunately, they did not look under the bed, or they would have seen a large plate piled with appetising dainties. They went away with threatening murmurs in which the word 'tomorrow' figured largely.

When they had gone William got out of bed with great caution and sat in the darkness munching iced cakes.

That sleep idea had been jolly good. Of course, he knew it couldn't go on indefinitely. He couldn't go on sleeping for a month. He'd have to wake up tomorrow, but tomorrow was tomorrow, and when tonight holds an entire plate of iced cakes (many of them with layers of real cream inside), tomorrow is hardly worth serious consideration.

CHAPTER 5

WiLLiAM JOiNS THE WAiTS

It was only two days before Christmas and the Outlaws stood in Ginger's back garden discussing its prospects, somewhat pessimistically. All except Henry – for Henry, in a spirit of gloomy resignation to fate, had gone to spend the festival season with relations in the North.

'What're *you* goin' to get?' demanded William of Ginger. The Outlaws generally spent the week before Christmas in ascertaining exactly what were the prospects of that day. It was quite an easy task, owing chiefly to the conservative habits of their relatives in concealing their presents in the same place year after year. The Outlaws knew exactly in which drawer or cupboard to pursue their search, and could always tell by some unerring instinct which of the concealed presents was meant for them.

'Nothin' really *'citin'*,' said Ginger, without enthusiasm, 'but nothin' *awful*, 'cept what Uncle George's giv'n me.'

'What's that?' said William.

'An ole *book*,' said Ginger with withering contempt; 'an ole book called *Kings an' Queens of England*. Huh! An' I shall have to say I like it an' thank him an' all that. An' I shan't be able to sell it even, 'cept for about sixpence, 'cause you never can, an' it cost five shillin's. *Five shillin's!* It's got five shillin's on the back. Well, why can't he give me the five shillin's an' let me buy somethin' sensible?'

He spoke with the bitterness of one who airs a grievance of long standing. 'Goin' wastin' their money on things like *Kings an' Queens of England*, 'stead of giv'n it to us to buy somethin' sensible. Think of all the sensible things we could buy with five shillin's – 'stead of stupid things like *Kings an' Queens of England*.'

'Well,' burst out Douglas indignantly. 'S'not so bad as what my Aunt Jane's got for me. She's gotter ole tie. *A tie!*' He spat the word out with disgust. 'I found it when I went to tea with her las' week. A silly ole green tie. Well, I'd rather pretend to be pleased over any ole book than over a silly green tie. An' I can't even sell it, 'cause they'll keep

109

goin' on at me to wear it – a sick'nin' ole green tie!'

William was not to be outdone.

'Well, you don't know what my Uncle Charles is givin' me. I heard him tellin' mother about it. A silly baby penknife.'

'A penknife!' they echoed. 'Well, there's nothin' wrong with a penknife.'

'I'd rather have a penknife than an old *Kings an' Queens of England*,' said Ginger bitterly.

'An' I'd rather have a penknife *or* a *Kings an' Queens of England* than a silly ole green tie,' said Douglas.

'A *Kings an' Queens of England*'s worse than a tie,' said Ginger fiercely, as though his honour were involved in any suggestion to the contrary.

''Tisn't!' said Douglas equally fiercely.

''Tis!' said Ginger.

''Tisn't!' said Douglas.

The matter would have been settled one way or the other by physical contest between the protagonists had not William thrust his penknife (metaphorically speaking) again into the discussion.

'Yes,' he said, 'but you don't know what *kind* of a

penknife, an' I do. I've got three penknives, an' one's almost as big as a nornery knife, an' got four blades *an'* a thing for taking stones out of horses' hoofs *an'* some things what I haven't found out what they're meant for yet, an' this what he's given me is a baby penknife – it's only got one blade, an' I heard him tellin' mother that I couldn't do any harm with it. Fancy,' – his voice quivered with indignation – '*fancy* anyone givin' you a penknife what you can't do any harm with.'

Ginger and Douglas stood equally aghast at this news. The insult of the tie and the *Kings and Queens of England* paled before the deadly insult of a penknife you couldn't do any harm with.

William returned home still burning with fury.

He found his mother in the drawing-room. She looked rather worried.

'William,' she said, 'Mr Solomon's just been here.'

William heard the news without much interest. Mr Solomon was the superintendent of the Sunday School, on which the Outlaws reluctantly shed the light of their presence every Sunday afternoon. Mr Solomon was very young and earnest and well-meaning, and the Outlaws found it generally quite easy to ignore him. He in his official capacity found it less easy to ignore the Outlaws. But he was an ever hopeful man, and never gave up his efforts to reach their better selves, a part of them which had hitherto succeeded in eluding him.

'He's going to take the elder boys out carol singing on Christmas Eve,' went on Mrs Brown uncertainly. 'He came to ask whether I'd rather you didn't go.'

William was silent. The suggestion was entirely unexpected and full of glorious possibilities. But, as he understood well enough the uncertainty in his mother's voice, he received it without any change of expression. The slight disgust, caused by brooding over the ignominy of a penknife he couldn't do any harm with, remained upon his unclassic features.

'Uh-huh?' he said with interest.

'Would you like to go?' said Mrs Brown.

'Wouldn't mind,' said William casually, his expression of disgust giving way to one of mere boredom. Mrs Brown, watching him, thought that Mr Solomon's apprehensions were quite ill-founded.

'If you went, William,' she said, 'you'd be quite quiet

and orderly, wouldn't you?'

William's expression was one of amazement. He looked as though he could hardly credit his ears.

'*Me?*' he said indignantly. '*Me?* – why, of *course*!'

He seemed so hurt by the question that his mother hastened to reassure him.

'I thought you would, dear. I told Mr Solomon you would. You – you'd like it, wouldn't you, dear?'

'Uh-huh,' said William, careful not to sound too eager.

'What would you like about it, dear?' asked Mrs Brown, priding herself upon her cunning.

William assumed an unctuous expression.

'Singin' hymns an' – an' psalms,' he said piously, 'an' – an' that sort of thing.'

His mother looked relieved.

'That's right, dear,' she said. 'I think it would be a very beautiful experience for you. I told Mr Solomon so. He seemed afraid that you might go in the wrong spirit, but I told him that I was sure you wouldn't.'

Mrs Brown's unquenchable faith in her younger son was one of the most beautiful and touching things the world has ever known.

'Oh, no,' said William, looking deeply shocked at the notion. 'I won't go in the wrong spirit, I'll go in, you know – what you said – a beautiful experience an' all that sort of spirit.'

'Yes,' agreed Mrs Brown, 'I'd like you to go. It will be the sort of experience you'll remember all your life.'

As a matter of fact it turned out to be the sort of experience that Mr Solomon rather than William remembered all his life.

William met Ginger and Douglas the next morning.

'I'm goin' waitin' Christmas Eve,' he announced proudly.

'So'm I,' said Ginger.

'So'm I,' said Douglas.

It turned out that Mr Solomon had visited their parents too, yesterday, and to their parents, too, had expressed doubt as to the advisability of their sons being allowed to join the party. Though well meaning, he was not a very tactful young man, and had not expressed his doubts in such a way as to placate maternal pride.

'My mother said,' said Ginger, 'why shun't I go same as anyone else, so I'm goin'!'

'So did mine,' said Douglas, 'so so'm I.'

'Yes,' said William indignantly, 'fancy sayin' he thought I'd better not come. Why, I should think I'm 's good at waitin' 's anybody else in the world – why, when I start singin' you c'n hear me at the other end of the village.'

This statement, being unassailable, passed unchallenged.

'Do you know where we're goin'?' continued William.

'He said beginnin' up Well Lane' said Douglas.

'My Uncle George lives in Well Lane,' said Ginger thoughtfully, 'the one what's givin' me *Kings an' Queens of England.*'

There was a short silence. In that silence the thought came to all three Outlaws that the expedition might have even vaster possibilities than at first they had imagined.

'*Then*, where we goin'?' said William.

'Jus' up the village street,' said Douglas.

'My Uncle Charles,' said William thoughtfully, 'the one what's givin' me the penknife you can't do any harm with, lives right away from the village.'

'So does my Aunt Jane – the one what's givin' me the ole green tie.'

William's face assumed its expression of daring leadership.

'Well,' he said, 'we'll jus' have to do what we can.'

Many, many times before Christmas Eve arrived did Mr Solomon bitterly regret the impulse on which he had suggested his party of waits. He would have liked to cancel the arrangement altogether, but he lacked the courage.

He held several practices in which his party of full-voiced but unmelodious musicians roared 'Good King Wenceslas' and 'The First Noel', making up in volume for what they lacked in tone and technique. During these practices he watched the Outlaws apprehensively. His apprehensions increased as time went on, for the Outlaws were behaving like creatures from another and a higher world.

They were docile and obedient and respectful. And this was not normal in the Outlaws. Normally they would by now have tired of the whole thing. Normally they would be clustered in the back row cracking nuts and throwing the shells at friends or foes. But they were not. They were standing in the front row wearing saintly expressions (as far, that is, as the expressions of the Outlaws could convey the idea of saintliness), singing 'Good King Wenceslas

Looked Out' with strident conscientiousness.

Mr Solomon would have been relieved to see them cracking nuts or deliberately introducing discords into the melody (they introduced discords, it is true, but unconsciously). He began to have a horrible suspicion that they were forming some secret plan.

The prospective waits assembled with Mr Solomon at the end of the village at nightfall. Mr Solomon was intensely nervous. It had taken all his better self to resist the temptation to put the whole thing off on the fictitious excuse of sudden illness. He held a lantern in his hand and a large tin of sweets under his arm. He had bought the large tin of sweets last night on the spur of the moment. He had a vague hope that it might prove useful in some crisis.

He raised the lantern and examined the little crowd of faces around him. He looked as though he were counting them. In reality he was anxiously ascertaining whether the Outlaws were there. He'd been clinging all day to the hope that the Outlaws mightn't be there. After all, he had thought hopefully, there was quite a lot of measles about. Or they might have forgotten. But his heart sank. There they were, standing in the very centre of the group. He sighed. Probably there were hundreds of boys all over the world coming out in rashes at that moment, and yet here were these boys as bloomingly healthy as they'd ever been. Life was full of irony.

'Well, here we are,' he said in that voice of rather painful brightness that he always used with the young. 'Here we all are . . . All got your best voices, eh? Now we'll go down Well Lane first.'

'Uncle George,' whispered Ginger.

'Go straight down the lane,' said Mr Solomon, 'till you get to the Laurels, and then turn in and we'll begin with "The First Noel".'

Obediently the little troupe set off towards Well Lane. It was as quiet and good and orderly as a Sunday School superintendent's heart could wish, and yet the Sunday School superintendent's heart was not quite light. He could not help remembering the proverbial order of sequence of the calm and the storm.

He'd have felt, of course, quite happy if the Outlaws hadn't been there.

He had, however, taken quite a lot of trouble over the

itinerary. He meant only to pay half-a-dozen visits, and to sing only one carol at each. It was not likely that they would receive any encores. The whole thing ought to be over in an hour. He hoped it would be, anyway.

He had already prepared the householders who were to be honoured by a visit from his waits, and though not enthusiastic they were ready to receive the visitants in a Christmas spirit of good will. He meant to risk no unchristian reception by paying unexpected visits. Though he was well-meaning rather than musical still he had a vague suspicion that the performance of his choir left a good deal to be desired.

The Misses Perkins lived at the Laurels, and they had assured Mr Solomon that they would love – simply *love* – to hear the dear little boys sing Christmas carols, and so would Muffy. (Muffy was the Misses Perkins' cat.) The visit to the Misses Perkins, anyway, ought to go off nicely. Fortunately, the Misses Perkins were slightly deaf.

Everything seemed to be going off very nicely so far. The waits were walking quietly and sedately down the road, not shouting or fighting as boys so often did. Mr Solomon's spirits rose. It was really after all a very beautiful idea –

and they were really after all very nice boys. He could see William and Ginger and Douglas walking decorously and silently together. Marvellous how even such boys as those yielded to the Christmas spirit.

They were walking at the head, leading the little troupe; they were turning obediently in at the gate of the Laurels. The young man took out his tuning fork and followed, smiling proudly.

Then the light of his lantern shone upon the gate as he entered and – it wasn't the Laurels.

They'd made a mistake. It wasn't the Laurels. It was the Cedars.

Mr Solomon, of course, could not know that the Outlaws had passed the Laurels and entered the Cedars deliberately because Ginger's Uncle George lived at the Cedars.

'Come back!' called Mr Solomon's thin voice through the night. 'It's the wrong house! Come back!'

But already the waits had burst violently into 'The First Noel'. It was a pity that they did not wait for the note from Mr Solomon, who had his tuning fork already in his hand.

It was a pity that they did not begin all together, and that having begun each at a separate moment each should cling so tenaciously to his own time and interpretation. It was a great pity that they did not know the words.

It was the greatest pity of all that they possessed the voices they did possess. But there is no denying their zest. There is no denying that each one put all the power and energy he possessed into his rendering of the carol. The resulting sound was diabolical. Diabolical is a strong word, but it is hardly strong enough. The English language does not really possess a word strong enough to describe the effect of these waits' rendering of 'The First Noel'.

After one minute of it, Uncle George's window was flung up and Uncle George's purple face was thrust out.

'Go away, you young devils!' he sputtered. 'How *dare* you come here kicking up that infernal din? Go a-*way*, I say!'

Mr Solomon's voice in the rear kept up its shrill but ineffective plaint.

'Come away, boys – it's the wrong house. I said the Laurels – the Misses Perkins and Muffy will be wondering wherever we are – quietly, boys – don't *shout* so – and you've got the wrong note—'

But nobody heard him. The uproar continued to be

deafening. The other waits realised that the Outlaws were for some reason or other determined to make as much noise as possible and gladly gave their assistance. They found the process exhilarating. They began to think that

'GO AWAY, YOU YOUNG DEVILS!' HE SPLUTTERED.
'HOW DARE YOU COME KICKING UP THAT DIN.'

the whole affair was going to be more interesting than they had thought it would be. Joyfully they yelled and yelled and yelled. Above them the purple-faced figure of Uncle George gesticulated and uttered words which were (fortunately,

MR SOLOMON'S VOICE IN THE REAR KEPT UP ITS SHRILL PLAINT. 'COME AWAY, BOYS! IT'S THE WRONG HOUSE!'

perhaps) drowned by the inferno of sound below.

Then, suddenly, silence came. Abruptly the Outlaws had stopped singing and the others at once stopped too, waiting developments. It was, of course, Uncle George's chance, and the immediate development was a flood of eloquence from Uncle George, to which the waits listened with joyful interest and at which Mr Solomon grew pale.

'Pardon me, sir,' gasped Mr Solomon, at last recovering. 'Quite a mistake – boys mistook house – visit meant for friends of ours – no offence intended, I assure you.'

But so breathless was he that only the two boys nearest him heard him, and no one heeded him. For to the amazement of all of them (except Ginger and Douglas), William spoke up firmly from the foreground.

'Please, sir, we're c'lectin' books for our library. Please sir, can you give us a book for our lib'ry?'

Mr Solomon gaped in open-mouthed amazement at this statement. He tried to utter some protest, but could only stutter.

Uncle George, however, could do more than stutter. He answered the question in the negative with such strength, and at such length, that the waits' admiration of him became a sort of ecstasy. William answered the refusal by bursting with amazing promptitude and discord into 'Good King Wenceslas'.

The Outlaws followed his lead. The rest of the waits joined in, most of them showing their conservative spirits by clinging still to 'The First Noel'. Not that it mattered much. No listener could have told what any of them was singing. Words and tune were lost in a tornado of unmelodious sound. Each wait tasted the rapture of exerting the utmost force of his lungs, and trying to drown his neighbour's effort.

In front of them Uncle George hung out of his bedroom window gesticulating violently, his complexion changing from purple to black.

Behind them Mr Solomon clung to the gatepost of the Cedars, moaning softly and mopping his brow.

A second time the waits stopped suddenly at a signal from William. The nightmare sound died away and there followed a silence broken only by the moans of Mr Solomon and sputtering from Uncle George, in which could be recognised the oft-returning words 'the police'.

But something of Uncle George's first fine careless frenzy

was gone. There was something broken about him, as there would indeed have been something broken about anyone who had listened to the ghastly sound. Again William spoke up brightly.

'Please c'n you give us a book for our lib'ry? We're collectin' books for our lib'ry. We want a book for boys – 'bout history, please. If you've got one to give us. For our lib'ry please.'

In the background, Mr Solomon, still clinging to the gatepost, moaned. 'I assure you, sir – mistake – wrong house—'

With admirable promptness and a force that was amazing considering the energy that he must have already expended, William burst with sudden unexpected violence into 'Fight the Good Fight', which Mr Solomon had been teaching them the Sunday before. It was taken up by the others, each, as before, striking out an entirely independent line in his rendering of it. It was the last straw. Uncle George was beaten.

With an expression of agony he clapped his hands over his ears and staggered backwards. Then he reappeared, and *The Kings and Queens of England* hit William and fell on to the gravel at his feet. William picked it up and signalled that the hymn should cease. A moment later the waits had gone. There only remained Mr Solomon clinging to the gatepost, stupefied by the terrible events he had just lived through, and Uncle George sputtering at the open window.

Uncle George's sputtering suddenly ceased, and he hurled at Mr Solomon's figure, dimly perceived through the darkness, a flood of eloquence which was worthy of a more discerning and appreciative audience.

Mr Solomon looked around him wildly. He looked for his lantern. It was gone. He looked for his tin of sweets. It was gone. He looked for his waits. They were gone.

Pursued by Uncle George's lurid invective he fled into the road and looked up and down it. There was no sign of lantern or tin of sweets or waits. He tore along to the village street where he had told them to go next and where presumably their next warned host awaited them.

There was no sign of them.

Distracted he tore up and down the road.

Then at the end of the road there appeared the tall burly figure of – a policeman. Unstrung by his experience, the blameless Mr Solomon fled from the minion of the law like a criminal and ran as fast as his legs could carry him homewards.

Meanwhile the waits were joyfully approaching the house of Douglas's Aunt Jane on the hillside. William swaggered at the head of them, carrying the lantern in one hand and the tin of sweets in the other. Behind him followed the others, each sucking happily a mouthful of sweets.

Kings and Queens of England had been flung into the village stream on the way. None of them except the Outlaws knew what it was all about. All they knew was that what had promised to be a dull and lawful expedition, organised by the Sunday School authorities, was turning out to be a thrilling and lawless expedition organised by William.

They followed him gladly, thinking blissfully of that glorious medley of sounds at which they had assisted, looking forward to another, and enjoying the delightful experience of having their mouths filled to their utmost capacity with Mr Solomon's sweets.

William led them into the garden of Rose Cottage, where Douglas's Aunt Jane lived. There they massed themselves ready for the onslaught. Those who had not finished their sweets swallowed them whole, and all drew in their breath.

They looked at William. William gave the signal. The outburst came. The effect was more powerful even than before, because no two of them were singing the same tune.

William, tiring of carols, was singing 'Valencia' at the top of his voice.

Ginger, who had not moved with the times, was singing 'Yes, We Have No Bananas'.

Douglas was still singing 'Good King Wenceslas'.

Of the others, one was singing 'D'ye Ken John Peel?' and others were singing 'Fight the Good Fight', 'The First Noel', 'Tea for Two', and 'Here We Are Again'. They all sang with gusto.

They had been singing for nearly ten minutes, when Douglas stopped them with an imperious gesture.

'I say,' he said to William, 'I forgot – she's deaf.'

The Outlaws were obviously nonplussed by this. They stared blankly, first at Douglas, then at his aunt's house. Suddenly Ginger said excitedly, 'Look! She's come downstairs.'

Certainly a lighted candle could be seen moving about in the downstairs room where before all had been darkness.

'Well,' said Douglas simply. 'I'm not goin' away without that tie now we've come this far for it.'

'I'll go,' volunteered William, 'an' see if I can get it off her. You'd better not, 'cause she knows you – go on singin', the rest of you.'

With that William advanced boldly into the enemy's country. He had no clear idea of what he was going to do. He would simply await the inspiration of the moment which so seldom failed him.

He was afraid that the deaf old lady would not hear his knock, but she opened to him almost immediately and dragged him within with a suddenness that amazed and perturbed him. There was something witch-like about her as she stood, tall and gaunt, her grey hair over her shoulders, wrapped in a long grey dressing-gown. She held an ear-trumpet in one hand.

'Come in!' she said excitedly. 'Come in! Come in! Saw you coming through the window – What is it?'

She held out her trumpet to him and he repeated into it nervously: 'What's what?'

'That sound,' she went on. 'It roused me from sleep; the roaring of wild animals or – is it an air raid?

Has some enemy attacked us?'

'No,' William hastened to assure her through the trumpet, 'it's not that.'

'Animals, then,' she went on, still excited; 'it sounded to me like the baying of wolves. Did you see them?'

'Yes,' said William into the trumpet.

'And came here for protection? I thought so – they must have escaped from the circus at Moncton. I heard that there was a pack of live wolves there – most dangerous, I've always thought, this exhibiting of wild animals – are they round the house, boy? Listen!'

Outside arose the glorious medley of 'The First Noel', 'Good King Wenceslas', 'Fight the Good Fight', 'D'ye Ken John Peel?', 'Yes, We Have No Bananas', 'Tea for Two', and 'Here We Are Again'.

Aunt Jane shuddered.

'All round the house,' she said. 'Even I can hear it, a most blood-curdling sound. I have often read of it, but never thought that it would fall to my lot to hear it. The first thing to do is to barricade the house.'

William, slightly bewildered by the turn events had taken, watched her move a table across the window and block up the door with a tall cupboard.

'There!' she said at last. 'That should keep them away. And I have provisions for several days.'

Aunt Jane seemed almost stimulated by the thought of the pack of wolves howling around her lonely hillside house.

'Listen,' she said again as the hideous uproar outside continued. 'Listen and imagine the tawny brutes with ravening open fangs. Listen to that,' as Ginger's strong young voice proclaimed above the general uproar that he had no bananas. 'Did you hear? – that voice speaks of greed and cunning, of lust for blood and a passionate hatred of the human race.'

As she spoke she moved to and fro, moving pieces of furniture across doors and windows.

William was utterly at a loss. He didn't know what to do or say. He watched her in open-mouthed bewilderment. Whenever he looked as if he were going to speak she placed the ear-trumpet in place for him so much that he gave a sickly smile and shook his head.

He watched her blocking up every available entrance to her cottage and wondered desperately how on earth he was

'HAS SOME ENEMY ATTACKED US?' SHE ASKED.
'NO!' WILLIAM ASSURED HER THROUGH THE TRUMPET.

going to get out of it. He wished to goodness that he'd never come in – that he'd let Douglas get his own silly tie. The waits outside were chanting as merrily and discordantly as ever.

Suddenly Aunt Jane left the room to reappear triumphantly a few minutes later carrying a large and old-fashioned gun.

'It's a long time since I used it,' she said, 'but I believe it might get one or two of them.'

William's annoyance turned to dismay.

'Oh, I wouldn't. I – er – wouldn't,' he protested.

She could not hear what he said, but seeing his lips move she presented him with the other end of her ear-trumpet.

'What do you say?'

He gave his sickly grin.

'Er – nothing,' he said.

'Then I wish you'd stop saying nothing,' she said tartly. 'If you've anything to say, *say* it, and if you haven't, *don't*, instead of mumbling away there and saying you're saying nothing.'

William gave her the sickly smile again and blinked.

She clambered on to the table before the window and

opened the window very slightly. Through the small aperture thus made she projected the muzzle of her gun. William watched her, paralysed with horror. Outside the medley of song rose higher and higher.

William could dimly discern the forms of his companions through the darkness. Aunt Jane was as short-sighted as she was hard of hearing.

'I can see them,' she said eagerly. 'Dim, lean, sinister shapes out there – now I *really* think I might get one or two. Anyway, the sound of the shot might drive them farther off.'

William felt as though in a nightmare, powerless to move or to speak as the old lady pointed the deadly weapon at his unsuspecting friends chanting their varied repertoire of songs so merrily in the darkness. Then, before the fatal shot rang out, William plucked her dressing-gown. She turned to him irritably and held the ear-trumpet to him again.

'Well,' she snapped, 'what's the matter now? Got anything to say yet?'

William suddenly found both his voice and an inspiration.

'Let's keep the gun for a – for a sort of last resource,' he yelled into the trumpet, ''case they sort of attack the house.'

She was obviously impressed by the idea. She took in the gun, closed the window and descended from the table.

'Something in that,' she said.

The success of his inspiration restored William's self-

'I CAN SEE THEM,' SHE SAID EAGERLY.
'DIM, LEAN, SINISTER SHAPES OUT THERE.'

respect. Something of his dejection vanished and something of his swagger returned. Suddenly his face shone. An idea – an IDEA – an IDEA – had occurred to him.

'I say,' he gasped.

'Well?' she snapped.

'I've heard,' he yelled into the aperture, 'I've *heard* that wolves are frightened of green.'

'Of green?' she said irritably, 'of green what?'

'Jus' of green,' said William, 'of green colour.'

'What nonsense!' she snapped.

'Well, I've *heard* it,' persisted William. 'Heard of a man drivin' away a whole herd o' wolves by jus' goin' out and showin' 'em a green tablecloth.'

'Well, I've not got a green tablecloth, so that settles it.'

But William didn't think it did. 'Haven't you got *anythin'* green?' he persisted.

She considered.

'One or two small green things,' she said, 'but green varies so. What sort of green should it be?'

William considered this question in silence for a minute. Then, 'Can't quite describe it,' he yelled, 'but I'd know if I saw.'

That, he couldn't help thinking, was rather neat.

After a slight hesitation Aunt Jane went from the room and soon returned with an olive green scarf, a bottle green hat, and a new tie of a most virulent pea green.

William's eyes gleamed when they fell upon the tie.

'That's it!' he shouted. 'That's the green.'

Aunt Jane looked rather annoyed. 'I particularly wanted that for tomorrow,' she said peevishly, 'won't the scarf do? I've no further use for it.'

'No,' said William very decidedly, pointing to the tie, '*that's* the green.'

'All right,' she said, 'but it's too dark for them to see it.'

'I'll take a lantern. I've gotter lantern in the porch.'

'They'll attack you if you go out there.'

'Not if they see the green,' said William firmly.

'Very well,' said Aunt Jane, who was beginning to feel rather sleepy, 'take it if you like.'

William slipped out into the night with the green tie. Aunt Jane waited.

The noise outside died away, and all was silent.

Aunt Jane suspected that the boy had been devoured by the wolves, but the thought did not trouble her very much.

She merely strengthened her fortifications and then went to bed. There was something rather inhuman about Aunt Jane. There must have been something rather inhuman about anyone who could choose a tie that colour.

The green tie had been torn into a thousand pieces, and trodden into the ditch. The toffee tin was almost empty. The waits were growing sleepy. Their songs, though no less discordant than before, were beginning to lack verve. Only Uncle Charles remained to be dealt with. Headed by William they marched upon Uncle Charles's house. Boldly they surged into Uncle Charles's garden. There they stood and upraised their strong young voices, and sang. Uncle Charles's window was flung up as quickly as Uncle George's had been.

'Go away, you young rascals,' he boomed.

The singing ceased.

'Please, sir—'

In the meek falsetto Uncle Charles did not recognise his nephew William's voice.

'Go away, I tell you. You won't get a halfpenny out of me.'

'Please sir, we're trying to go, but I've got all caught up in the clothes-line what was out in the grass.'

'Well, uncatch yourself.'

'I can't.'

'Cut it, then, you young fool.'

'Please, sir, I haven't got a penknife.'

Uncle Charles cursed softly, and after a short silence a penknife struck Ginger's head and fell on to the lawn. William seized it eagerly and examined it. It was the one! It was the penknife he couldn't do any harm with.

'Cut yourself loose with that, you young scoundrels, and get off with you, disturbing people's rest like this – if it wasn't Christmas Eve I'd have the whole lot in jail. I'd—'

But the waits had gone. Sucking the last of the sweets and still singing horribly, they were marching back through the village.

It was the day after Christmas Day. William and Ginger and Douglas foregathered in Ginger's back garden. It was the first time they had met since Christmas Eve. Christmas Day had perforce been spent in the bosoms of their families.

'Well?' said William eagerly to Ginger.

'He didn't say anything about the book,' said Ginger. 'He jus' gave me five shillin's.'

'An' neither did she about the tie,' said Douglas, 'she jus' gave me five shillin's.'

As a matter of fact Aunt Jane had gone to a neighbour the next morning to pour out the wolf story, but the neighbour (who was boiling with that indignation which only a disturbed night can produce) got in first with the wait story, and after hearing it Aunt Jane had become very thoughtful and had decided to say nothing about the wolf story.

'Uncle Charles,' grinned William, 'said that some fools of choir boys got tied up in the clothes-line 'n' he'd thrown 'em the penknife he'd got for me 'n' they'd pinched it 'n' he gave me five shillings.'

Each of the three produced two half-crowns upon a grimy palm.

William sighed happily.

'Fifteen shillin's,' he said. 'Jus' *think* of it! *Fifteen shillin's!* Come on. Let's go down to the village an' spend it.'

CHAPTER 6

WiLLiAM PLAYS SANTA CLAUS

William walked slowly and thoughtfully down the village street. It was the week after Christmas. Henry was still away. Douglas and Ginger were the only two of his friends left in the village. Henry's absence had its bright side because Henry's father had, in the excitement of the departure, forgotten to lock his garage and the Outlaws found Henry's father's garage a nice change from the old barn, their usual meeting place. William was glad that Christmas was over. He'd not done badly out of it on the whole, but Christmas was a season too sacred to the conventions and to uncongenial relatives to appeal to William.

Suddenly he saw someone coming down the village street towards him. It was Mr Solomon, the superintendent of the Sunday School of which William was a reluctant but inglorious member. William had his reasons for not wishing to meet Mr Solomon. Mr Solomon had organised a party of waits for Christmas Eve from his Sunday School attendants and William had not only joined this party but had assumed leadership of it. They had managed to detach themselves from Mr Solomon quite early in the evening and had spent the night in glorious lawlessness. William had not seen Mr Solomon since that occasion because Mr Solomon had had a slight nervous breakdown and William was now torn between a desire to elude him and a desire to tackle him. The desire to elude him needs no explanation. The desire to tackle was equally simple. William had heard that Mr Solomon, who was ever prolific in fresh ideas, had decided to form a band from the elder boys of the Sunday School. It may be thought that Mr Solomon should have learnt wisdom from his experience on Christmas Eve but then Mr Solomon had decided to ensure success for his scheme by the simple process of debarring the Outlaws from it. William had heard of this and the news had filled him with such righteous indignation that it overcame even his natural reluctance to meet the organiser of the Christmas Eve carol party.

He confronted him squarely.

'Afternoon, Mr Solomon,' he said.

Mr Solomon looked him up and down with distaste.

'Good afternoon, my boy,' he said icily. 'I am on my way to pay a visit to your parents.'

This news was not encouraging. William turned to accompany him, consoled slightly by the knowledge that both his parents were out. Losing no time he boldly approached the subject of the band.

'Hear you're gettin' up a band, Mr Solomon,' he said casually.

'I am,' said Mr Solomon more icily than ever.

'I'd like to be a trumpeter,' said William, still casually.

'You have not been asked to join the band,' went on Mr Solomon with a firmness unusual in that mild young man, but his mind was still raw with the memories of Christmas Eve, 'and you will *not* be asked to join the band.'

'Oh,' said William politely.

'You may wonder,' went on Mr Solomon with deep emotion, 'why I am going to pay a visit to your parents.'

William didn't wonder at all, but he said nothing.

'I am going,' continued Mr Solomon, 'to complain to your parents of your shameful behaviour on Christmas Eve.'

'Oh – that,' said William as though he remembered the incident with difficulty. 'I remember – we – sort of lost you, didn't we? It's easy losin' people in the pitch dark. It made it very awkward for us,' he went on complainingly, 'you gettin' lost like that.'

'You are at liberty, of course,' said Mr Solomon, 'to give your version of the affair to your parents. I shall give mine. I have little doubt which they will believe.'

William also had little, or rather no doubt at all, which they would believe. He was constantly being amazed and horrified by his parents' lack of credulity in his versions of affairs. He changed the subject hastily.

'I could easily learn a trumpet,' he volunteered, 'an' so c'd Ginger·an' Douglas – an' Henry when he comes back an' – an' it won't be so easy to lose you with a band in daylight. It was with it bein' so dark that we sort of got lost Christmas Eve.'

Mr Solomon disdained to answer.

After a pause, William said solicitously, 'Sorry t'hear

you've been ill.'

'My slight indisposition,' said Mr Solomon, 'was the result of our ill-fated expedition on Christmas Eve.'

'Yes,' said William who was determined to cover that ill-fated expedition as far as possible with the cloak of innocency, 'it was a nasty cold night. I was sneezin' a bit myself the next mornin'.'

Again Mr Solomon disdained to answer.

'Well, when I'm in your band,' said William with his irrepressible optimism, 'playin' a trumpet—'

'William,' said Mr Solomon patiently, 'you will *not* be in my band playing anything. If your parents continue to send you to Sunday School after receiving my complaint, I must – er – endure it, but you will *not* be in my band. Nor will any of your friends.'

At the suggestion that his parents might not continue to send him to Sunday School after receiving Mr Solomon's complaint, William's spirits had risen only to drop again immediately at the reflection that they would be all the more likely to insist upon it. Mr Solomon, of course, looked upon his Sunday School as a glorious privilege to its attendants. William's parents looked upon it more simply as their

Sunday afternoon's rest. They would not be likely to put an end to William's attendance there on any consideration.

Mr Solomon turned in at the gate of William's home and William accompanied him with an air of courage that was, as I have said, derived solely from the knowledge that both his parents were out. Then taking a muttered farewell of his companion he went round to the side of the house. His companion went up the front steps and rang the front door bell.

William amused himself in the back garden for some time but keeping under strict observation the front drive where the baffled Mr Solomon must soon beat his retreat. But no baffled Mr Solomon appeared beating his retreat. Curiosity impelled William to creep cautiously up to the drawing-room window. There sat Mr Solomon, flushed and simpering, having tea with Ethel, William's grown-up sister. Of course – he'd forgotten that Ethel was at home. Ethel was evidently being very nice to Mr Solomon. Ethel happened to be in the temporary and, for her, very rare position of being without a male admirer on the spot. Everyone seemed to have gone away for Christmas. Her latest conquest, Rudolph Vernon, an exquisite young man quite worthy of his name, had left her almost in tears the week before to pay a Christmas visit to an aunt in the country from whom he had expectations. Mr Solomon was not of course a victim worthy of Ethel's bow and spear, but he was better than no one. She happened also to be suffering from a cold in her head which made any diversion welcome. Therefore she gave him tea and smiled upon him. He sat, blushing deeply and gazing in rapt adoration at her blue eyes and Titian red hair (for Ethel put every other girl for miles around in the 'also ran' class as far as looks were concerned). He had not even dared to tell her the real object of his visit lest it should prejudice her against him. William feasted his eyes upon the spectacle of the lately indignant Mr Solomon, now charmed and docile and, metaphorically speaking, eating out of Ethel's hand, then curiosity impelled him to come to yet closer quarters with the spectacle. He was anxious to ascertain whether the complaint had actually been lodged against him or whether Ethel's smiles had driven it completely out of Mr Solomon's mind. Though, generally speaking, he disapproved of Ethel as unduly exacting and trammelling to his free spirit, he was forced in justice to admit that there were times when she had her uses.

He went upstairs, performed a hasty and sketchy toilet, assumed his most guileless expression and entered the drawing-room. At his entrance Ethel's alluring smile gave way to an expression of annoyance and Mr Solomon's allured smile to one of sheepishness. But this reception had no effect upon William. William was not sensitive to shades of manner. He sat down upon a chair next to Mr Solomon with the expression of one who has every intention of remaining where he is for some time, and turned his guileless countenance from Ethel to Mr Solomon, from Mr Solomon to Ethel. Silence had fallen at his entrance but it was obvious that someone must say something soon.

'There you are, dear,' said Ethel without enthusiasm. 'Would you like some tea?'

'No, thank you,' said William.

'Mr Solomon has very kindly come to make sure that you're none the worse after your little outing on Christmas Eve.'

William turned his guileless countenance upon Mr Solomon. Mr Solomon went pink and nearly choked over his tea. Demoralised by Ethel's beauty and sweetness of manner he had indeed substituted for his intended complaint a kindly inquiry as to William's health after his exposure to the elements on Christmas Eve, but it was hard to have this repeated in William's hearing and beneath William's sardonic gaze. William made no comment on this statement.

'That's very kind of him, isn't it, William?' said Ethel rather sharply. 'You ought to thank him.'

William still eyed the embarrassed man unflinchingly.

'Thank you,' he said in a tone in which the embarrassed man perceived quite plainly mockery and scorn.

A silence fell. Ethel always found the presence of William disconcerting when she was engaged in charming an admirer. So did the admirer. But William sat on.

'Haven't you any homework to do, William?' said Ethel at last.

'No,' said William, 'it's holidays.'

'Wouldn't you like to go out and play then?'

'No, thank you,' said William.

Ethel wondered as she had wondered hundreds of times before why somebody didn't discipline that boy. It was painful to have to conceal her natural exasperation beneath a sweet smile for the benefit of the visitor.

'Aren't any of your friends expecting you, dear?' she said with overacted and unconvincing sweetness.

'No,' said William and continued to sit and stare in front of him.

Suddenly the clock struck five and Mr Solomon started up.

'Good heavens!' he said. 'I must go. I ought to have gone some time ago.'

'Why?' said Ethel. 'It's very early.'

'B-but I ought to have been there by five.'

'Where?' said Ethel.

'It's the Old Folks' Christmas party. I was to give the presents – the children's home party too – I should have been at the Old Folks to give their presents at five and with the children at half-past five. I'm afraid I shall be terribly late.'

He looked about frantically.

'Oh, but,' said Ethel beseechingly, 'can't someone else do it for you? It seems such a shame for you to have to run off as soon as you've come.'

He was a most conscientious young man, but he looked

WILLIAM SAT ON AND ON.
HE WAS NOT DISCONCERTED.

into Ethel's blue, blue eyes and was lost. He didn't care who gave away the presents to the Old Folks and the children. He didn't care whether anyone gave them away. All he

'HAVEN'T YOU ANY HOMEWORK TO DO, WILLIAM?'
SAID ETHEL AT LAST.

wanted to do was to sit in this room and be smiled upon by
Ethel. It came to him suddenly that he'd met his soul's mate
at last. He'd had no idea that the world contained anyone

so wonderful and charming and kind and clever.

'Isn't there anyone who'd do it for you?' said Ethel again sweetly.

He thought for a minute.

'Well, I'm sure the curate wouldn't mind doing it,' he said at last. 'I'm sure he wouldn't, I've often taken his Boys' Club for him.'

'Well, William could take the message to him, couldn't he?' said Ethel.

Glorious idea! It would kill two birds with one stone. It would prolong this wonderful *tête-à-tête* and get rid of this objectionable boy. Mr Solomon's spirits rose. He smiled upon William almost benignly.

'Yes – you'll do that, won't you, William?'

'Yes,' said William obligingly, 'cert'nly.'

'Listen very carefully to me then, dear boy,' said Mr Solomon in his best Sunday School superintendent manner. 'Go to Mr Greene's house and ask him if he'd be kind enough – don't forget to put it like that – to take over my duties for this afternoon as I'm – er – unable to attend to them myself. Tell him that the two sacks containing the gifts for the Old Folks' party and the childrens' party are in my rooms. The bigger of the two is the Old Folks' party presents. He'll find in my rooms, too, a Father Christmas costume which he should wear for giving the Old Folks' presents and a Pied Piper costume for giving the childrens' presents. It's a pretty custom I've instituted – to wear the Pied Piper costume for the children. Then they form a procession and I lead them round the room and the mothers watch, before I give them the presents. Ask him if he can very kindly – *don't* forget to say that, dear boy – take over these two duties for me this afternoon and ask him if he can't to let me know at once by telephone. If I hear nothing more I'll take for granted that it's all right. Do you quite understand, dear boy?'

'Yes,' said William.

William walked slowly down the road to Mr Solomon's rooms. He had decided after all *not* to trouble to call upon the curate. He had decided very kindly to perform Mr Solomon's two little duties himself. He was most anxious to be admitted to Mr Solomon's band as a trumpeter, and he thought that if Mr Solomon found his two little duties correctly performed by William while he was pursuing his acquaintance with William's engaging sister, his heart might be melted and he might admit William as a trumpeter to his band despite his experience of Christmas Eve. Moreover there is no denying that the two little duties themselves strongly appealed to William. There is no denying that the thought of dressing up as Father Christmas and the Pied Piper and distributing gifts to Old Folks and children appealed very strongly indeed to William's highly developed dramatic instinct.

Mr Solomon's housekeeper admitted him without question. She was used to Mr Solomon's sending people of all ages and all classes to his rooms on various errands. She was annoyed at the marks William's muddy boots made on the hall that she'd just cleaned, but beyond remarking bitterly that some people didn't seem to know what mats was made for, she took no further notice of him. A few minutes later William might have been observed staggering across from Mr Solomon's rooms to the School with two large sacks and two large bundles over his shoulders.

He found a small classroom to change in. It was intensely thrilling to put on Father Christmas's beard and wig and the trailing red cloak edged with cotton wool.

He then carefully considered the two sacks. The larger of the two, Mr Solomon had said, was to be for the Old Folks, but William didn't approve of this at all. Why should the Old Folks have a larger sack than the children? William's sympathies were all on the side of the children. He shouldered the smaller sack therefore and set off to find the Old Folks' Party. As both parties were being held in the same building the corridors were freely adorned with placards pointing out the way by means of hands whose execution revealed much good intention, but little knowledge of anatomy. William easily tracked down the Old Folks' party. He listened for a moment outside the door to the confused murmur within, then flew open the door and entered dramatically. Old Folks in various stages of old age sat round the room talking to each other complainingly. A perspiring young man and woman were trying ineffectively to get them to join in a game. The guests were engaged in discussing among themselves the inadequacy of the tea and the uncomfortableness of the chairs and the piercingness of the draught and the general dullness of the party.

''Tisn't what it used to be in my young days,' one old man was saying loudly to his neighbours.

William entered with his sack.

At the sight of him they brightened.

The perspiring young man and woman hurried down to him eagerly.

'*So* glad to see you,' they gasped, 'you're awfully late – I suppose Mr Solomon sent you with the things?'

Not much of William's face could be seen through the all-enveloping beard and wig, but what could be seen signified assent.

'Well, do begin to give them out,' said the young man. 'It's simply ghastly! We can't get any *go* into it at all. They won't do anything but sit round and grumble. I hope you've got plenty of tea and 'baccy. That's what they like best. Are you going to make a speech?'

William hastily shook his head and lowered his sack from his shoulder.

'Well, begin at this end, will you? And let's hope to goodness that it'll cheer them up.'

William began and it was not until he had presented an amazed and outraged old man with a toy engine that it occurred to him that it had been perhaps a mistake to exchange the two sacks. But having begun, he went doggedly on with his task. He presented to the old men and women around him dolls and small tin motor cars and miniature shops and little wooden boats and garish little picture books and pencil cases – all presents laboriously chosen by the worthy Mr Solomon for the children. It was evident that the young man and woman helpers were restraining themselves with difficulty. The Old Folks were for the time being paralysed by amazement and indignation. Yet a close observer might have remarked that there was something of satisfaction in their indignation. They'd grumbled at the tea and room and chairs and draught till they were tired of grumbling at them. Something fresh to grumble at was almost in the nature of a godsend. Of course they'd have grumbled at their presents whatever they'd been, but anything so unusually and satisfactorily easy to grumble at as these unsuitable presents was almost exhilarating. William gathered from the almost homicidal expressions with which the young man and woman helpers were watching him that it would be as well to retire as hastily as possible. He handed his last present, a child's paintbox, to a deaf and blind old woman by the door, and departed almost precipitately. Then the storm broke out and a torrent of shrill indignation pursued his retreating form. He returned to the little classroom he had chosen as his dressing-room and stood contemplating his other costume and other sack. Yes, impersonally and impartially he could not help admitting that the changing of the sacks had been a mistake, but it was done now and he must carry on as best as he could. It took some time to change into the Pied Piper costume and he retained his beard and wig in order the better to conceal his identity. Then he shouldered his other sack and set off to follow the numerous placards whose hands crippled apparently by rheumatism or some other terrible complaint continued with dogged British determination to do their duty and point the way to the room where the children were assembled. William had become very thoughtful. He was realising the fact that in all probability his fulfilment of Mr Solomon's roles that afternoon would not be such as to melt Mr Solomon's heart towards him and make him admit him as trumpeter into his band. He doubted if even Ethel's charm would be strong enough to counter-balance the Old Folks' presents. And he did so dearly want to enter Mr Solomon's band as a trumpeter. He must try to think of some way. He flung open the door of a room in which a few dozen small children gambolled half-heartedly at the bidding of the conscientious 'helpers'. A little cluster of mothers sat at the end of the room and watched them proudly. The children, seeing him enter with his sack, brightened and instructed by the helpers, broke into a thin shrill cheer. A helper came down to greet him.

'How good of you to come,' she said gushingly. 'I suppose Mr Solomon couldn't get off himself. Such an indefatigable worker, isn't he? The procession first, of course – the children know just what to do – we've been rehearsing it.'

The children were already getting into line. The 'helper' motioned William to the head of it. William stepped into position.

'Twice round the room, you know,' said the helper, 'and then distribute the presents.'

William began very slowly to walk round the room, his sack on his shoulder, his train of children prancing joyously behind. William's brain was working quickly. He had not looked into the bag he was carrying, but he had a strong suspicion that he would soon be distributing packets of tea and tobacco to a gathering of outraged children. Surely the fury of the Old Folks presented with dolls and engines would be as nothing to the fury of children presented with packets of tea and tobacco. His hopes of being admitted into Mr Solomon's band faded into nothingness. He began his second peregrination of the room. Fond staff gazed in rapt admiration. William walked very slowly. He was trying to put off the evil hour when he must open the sack and take out the packets of tea and tobacco. Then suddenly he decided not to await meekly the blows of Fate. Instead he'd play a bold game. He'd carry the war into the enemy's country.

The mothers and helpers were surprised when suddenly William, followed by his faithful band (who would have died martyrs' deaths sooner than lose sight of that sack for one moment), walked out of the door and disappeared from view. But an intelligent helper smiled brightly and said:

'How thoughtful! He's just going to take them once round the School outside.'

'Perhaps,' suggested a mother, 'he's taken them for a peep at the Old Folks' party.'

'Who is he?' said another. 'I thought Mr Solomon was to have come.'

'Oh, it's probably one of Mr Solomon's elder Sunday School boys. He told me once that he believed in training them up in habits of social service. He's a *wonderful* man, I think.'

'Isn't he?' sighed another. '*Lives* for duty – I'm so sorry he couldn't come today.'

'Well, I'm sure,' said the first, 'he'd have come if some more pressing duty hadn't detained him. The dear man's probably reading to some poor invalid at this moment.'

At that moment as a matter of fact the dear man had got to the point where he was earnestly informing Ethel that no one had ever – ever – *ever* understood him in all his life before as she did.

'I don't think that Johnnie ought to have gone out of doors,' complained a mother. 'He hadn't got his chest protector on.'

'It's only for a second,' said a helper soothingly. 'It will air the room a bit.'

'But it won't put Johnnie's chest protector on,' said the mother pugnaciously. 'And what's the use of airing the room when we'd only just got it nice and warm for them.'

'I'll go out and see where they are,' said the helper

obligingly. She went out and looked round the School playground. The School playground was empty. She walked round to the other side of the School. There was no one there. There was no sign of anyone anywhere. She returned to the mothers and other helpers.

'They must have gone to see the Old Folks' party,' she said.

'If they're not outside,' said Johnnie's mother, 'I don't mind. All I meant was that if he was outside he ought to be wearing his chest protector.'

'I think,' said another helper rather haughtily, 'that that boy ought to have *told* us that he was going to take them to see the Old Folks. When I offer to help at a party I like to be consulted about the arrangements.'

'Well, let's go and find them,' said Johnnie's mother. 'I don't want Johnnie wandering about these nasty draughty passages without it. I wish now that I'd never taken it off.'

They set off in a body to the room where the Old Folks' party was being held. The Old Folks, sitting round the room, still held their little dolls or engines and toy boats, and were grumbling to each other about them with morbid relish. One helper was at the piano singing a cheerful little song to which no one was listening. The other was bending over an octogenarian, who despite himself was becoming interested in the workings of his clockwork bus. This interest, however, was disapproved of by the rest.

'Disgustin', I call it!' an old man was saying to his neighbour holding out the toy train signal with which William had presented him.

The neighbour, who was tired of talking about his toy mouse, glared ferociously at the performer.

'Kickin' up such a din a body can't hear himself speak,' he muttered.

The mothers and helpers of the children looked around anxiously, then swept up to the helpers of the Old Folks. A hasty whispered consultation took place. No, the Pied Piper and children had not visited them at all. Probably they had returned to their own rooms by now. The mothers and helpers hurried back to the room. It was still empty. Talking excitedly they poured out into the playground. It was empty. They poured out into the street. It was empty. Part of them tore frenziedly up the street and part tore equally frenziedly to search the building again. Everything was empty. The old legend had come true. A Pied Piper followed by every child in the village had vanished completely from the face of the earth.

Ethel had just sneezed and Mr Solomon was just thinking how much more musically she sneezed than anyone else he had ever met, when the mothers and helpers burst in upon them. The helpers took in the situation at a glance, and never again did Mr Solomon recapture the pedestal from which that glance deposed him. But that is by the way. The immediate question was the children. The babel was so deafening that it took a long time before Mr Solomon grasped what it was all about. Johnnie's mother had a penetrating voice, and for a long time Mr Solomon thought that all they had come to say was that Johnnie had lost his chest protector. When the situation finally dawned on him he blinked with horror and amazement.

'B-b-but Mr Greene came to give the presents,' he gasped. 'It was Mr Greene.'

'It certainly wasn't Mr Greene,' said a helper tartly. 'It was a boy. We thought it must have been one of your Sunday School boys. We couldn't see his face plainly because of his beard.'

A feeling of horror stole over Mr Solomon.

'A b-b-boy?' he gasped.

'If I'd known he was going out like that,' wailed Johnnie's mother, 'I'd never have taken it off.'

'Wait a minute,' stammered Mr Solomon excitedly, 'I-I'll go and speak to Mr Greene.'

But the visit to Mr Greene was entirely fruitless of missing children. All it produced was the information that Mr Greene had been out all the afternoon and had received no message of any kind from Mr Solomon.

'They – they can't really have gone,' said Mr Solomon. 'Perhaps they are hiding in some other classroom for a joke.'

With a crowd of distracted mothers at his heels he returned to the School and conducted there a thorough and systematic search. Though thorough and systematic as a search could be, it revealed no children. The attitude of the mothers was growing hostile. They evidently looked upon Mr Solomon as solely responsible for the calamity.

'Sittin' there,' muttered a mother fiercely, 'sittin' there dallyin' with red-haired females while our children was bein' stole – *Nero*!'

''*Erod!*' said another not to be outdone in general culture.

'*Crippen!*' said another showing herself more up-to-date.

The perspiration was pouring from Mr Solomon's brow. It was like a nightmare. He could not move anywhere without this crowd of hostile, muttering women. He had a horrible suspicion that they were going to lynch him, hang him from the nearest lamp-post. And what, oh what, in the name of St George's Hall, had happened to the children?

'Let us just look up and down the road again,' he said hoarsely. Still muttering darkly they followed him into the road. He looked up and down it wildly. There wasn't a child to be seen anywhere. The threatening murmurs behind him grew louder.

'Duck him,' he heard and 'Hangin's too good for him,' and 'Wring his neck with my own hands I will if he doesn't find 'em soon,' and from Johnnie's mother: 'Well, if I find him again it'll be a lesson to me never to take it off no more.'

'I-I'll go and look round the village,' said poor Mr Solomon desperately, 'I'll go to the police – I promise I'll find them.'

'You'd better,' said someone darkly.

He tore in panic down the road. He tore in panic up the nearest street. And then suddenly he saw William's face looking at him over a garden gate.

'Hello,' said William.

'Do you know anything about those children?' panted Mr Solomon.

'Yes,' said William calmly. 'If you promise to let me be a trumpeter in your band, you can have them. Will you?'

'Y-yes,' spluttered Mr Solomon.

'On your honour?' persisted William.

'Yes,' said Mr Solomon.

'An' Ginger an' Henry an' Douglas – all trumpeters?'

'Yes,' said Mr Solomon desperately. It was at that moment that Mr Solomon decided that not even Ethel's charm would compensate for having William for a brother-in-law.

'All right,' said William. 'Come round here.'

He led him round to a garage at the back of the house and opened the door. The garage was full of children having the time of their lives, engaged in mimic warfare under the leadership of Ginger and Douglas with ammunition of tea leaves and tobacco. Certainly the children were appreciating the Old Folks' presents far more than the Old Folks had appreciated the children's.

Johnnie, the largest and healthiest of the children, was engaged in chewing tobacco and evidently enjoying it.

'Here they are,' said William carelessly. 'You can have 'em if you like. We're gettin' a bit tired of them.'

No words of mine could describe the touching reunion between the mothers of the missing children and the children, or between Johnnie and his chest protector.

Neither could any words of mine describe the first practice of Mr

'HERE THEY ARE,' SAID WILLIAM. 'YOU CAN HAVE 'EM IF YOU LIKE.'

Solomon's Sunday School band with William, Ginger and Douglas and Henry as trumpeters.

There was, however, only one practice, as after that Mr Solomon wisely decided to go away for a very long holiday.

THE GARAGE WAS FULL OF CHILDREN
HAVING THE TIME OF THEIR LIVES.

CHAPTER 7

THE CHRISTMAS TRUCE

It was Hubert's mother's idea that the Outlaws versus Hubert Laneites feud should be abolished.

'Christmas, you know,' she said vaguely to William's mother, 'the season of peace and goodwill. If they don't bury the hatchet at this season they never will. It's so absurd for them to go on like this. Think how much *happier* they'd be if they were *friends*.'

Mrs Brown thought, murmured 'Er – yes,' uncertainly, and added, 'I've *tried*, you know, but boys are so funny.'

'Yes,' said Mrs Lane earnestly (Mrs Lane was large and breathless and earnest and overdressed), 'but they're *very* sweet, aren't they? Hubie's *awfully* sweet. I simply can't think how anyone could quarrel with Hubie. We'll make a *real* effort this Christmas to put an end to this foolish quarrel, won't we? I feel that if only your Willie got to know my Hubie properly, he'd simply love him, he would really. *Everyone* who really knows Hubie loves him.'

Mrs Brown said 'Er – yes,' still more uncertainly, and Mrs Lane continued: 'I've thought out how to do it. If you'll invite Hubie to Willie's party, we'll *insist* on his coming, and we'll invite Willie to Hubie's, and you *insist* on his coming, and then it will be all right. They'll have got to know each other, and, I'm sure, learnt to love each other.'

Mrs Brown said 'Er – yes,' more uncertainly than ever. She felt that Mrs Lane was being unduly optimistic, but still it *would* be nice to see the end of the feud that was always leading William into such wild and desperate adventures.

'Then we'll begin by—'

'Begin and end, my dear Mrs Brown,' said Mrs Lane earnestly, 'by making them attend each other's Christmas parties. I'm absolutely convinced that they'll *love* each other after that. I know anyway that Willie will love Hubie, because, when you really get to know Hubie, he's the most *lovable* boy you can possibly imagine.'

Mrs Brown said 'Er – yes,' again, because she couldn't think of anything else to say, and so the matter was settled.

When it was broached to William, he was speechless with horror.

'*Him?*' he exploded fiercely when at last the power of speech returned to him. 'Ask *him* to my Christmas party? I'd sooner not have a Christmas party at all than ask *him* to it. *Him!* Why I wun't go to the *King's* Christmas party, if *he* was going to be there. Not if I had to be beheaded for it. *Him?* Well, then I jolly well won't have a party at all.'

But Mrs Brown was unexpectedly firm. The overtures, she said, had come from Hubert's mother, and they could not with decency be rejected. It was the season of peace and goodwill ('No one's ever peaceful or goodwillin' to me at it,' put in William bitterly); and we must all bury the hatchet and start afresh.

'I don't want to bury no hatchet,' said William tempestuously, "cept in his head. *Him!* Wantin' to come to my party! *Cheek!*'

But William's tempestuous fury was as usual of no avail against his mother's gentle firmness.

'It's no use, William,' she said. 'I've *promised*. He's to come to your party, and you're to go to his, and Mrs Lane is quite sure that you'll be real friends after it.'

'*Me* friends with *him*!' exploded William. 'I'll never be friends with him—'

'But William,' said his mother, stemming his flood of frenzied oratory, 'I'm sure he's a very nice little boy when you get to know him.'

William replied to this by a (partially) dumb and very realistic show of physical nausea.

But faced by the alternative of Hubert Lane and his friends as guests at his party or no party at all, William bowed to the inevitable.

'All right,' he said, 'I'll have him then an' – all right, I won't *do* anythin' to him or to any of them, I'll wait till it's all over. I'll wait till he's been to my party an' I've been to his, an' then – well, you'll be jolly sorry you ever made us do it 'cause we'll have such a lot to make up.'

Mrs Brown, however, was content with her immediate victory. She sent an invitation to Hubert Lane and to Bertie Franks (Hubert's friend and lieutenant) and to Hubert's other friends, and they all accepted in their best copper-plate handwriting. William and his Outlaws went about sunk deep in gloom.

'If it wasn't for the trifle an' the crackers,' said William darkly, 'I wouldn't have had it at all – not with *him*. An' it'll have to be a jolly fine trifle, practic'ly *all* cream, to make it worth while.' His mood grew darker and darker as the day approached. He even discussed with his Outlaws the possibility of making a raid on the larder before the party, and carrying off trifles and jellies and fruit salad into the woods, leaving the Hubert Laneites to arrive and find the cupboard bare and their hosts flown. It was a tempting plan, but after dallying with it fondly for a few days they reluctantly gave it up, as being not really worth its inevitable consequences. Instead, they steeled themselves to go through the affair in the dogged spirit of martyrdom, their sufferings allayed only by the thought of the trifle and crackers, and the riot of hostilities that could take place as soon as the enforced Christmas truce was over. For the prospect of the end of the feud brought no glow of joy to the Outlaws' hearts. Without the Hubert Lane feud life would be dull indeed.

As the day of the party drew nearer, curiosity lightened the gloom of their spirits. How would the Hubert Laneites behave? Would they come reluctantly, surlily, at the bidding of authority, or would they come in a Christmas spirit of peace and goodwill, genuinely anxious to bury the hatchet? The latter possibility was too horrible to contemplate. Rather let them come in the spirit in which the Outlaws were prepared to receive them – a spirit in which one receives a deadly foe in time of truce, all their thoughts and energies centred on the happy moment when hostilities might be resumed.

William, of course, could not watch the preparations for his party and maintain unbroken his pose of aloof displeasure. The trifle was, he was convinced, the finest trifle that had yet been seen in the neighbourhood; there were jellies of every shape and hue, there was a cream blancmange decorated with cherries and angelica, and there was an enormous iced Christmas cake. *And* there were crackers. In the eyes of William and his friends it was the crackers that lent the final touch of festivity to the tea.

The Outlaws and their supporters, as arranged, arrived first, and stood around William like a bodyguard awaiting the arrival of the Hubert Laneites. They wore perfectly blank expressions, prepared to meet the Hubert Laneites in whatever guise they presented themselves. And the guise in which they ultimately presented themselves was worse than the Outlaws' worst fears. They were not surly foes, forced reluctantly to simulate neutrality, nor were they heralds of peace and goodwill. They advanced upon their host with an oily friendliness that was nauseating. They winked at each other openly. They said, 'Thanks *so* much for asking us, William. It was ripping of you. Oh, I say . . . what *topping* decorations!'

And they nudged each other and sniggered. William clenched his fists in his coat pocket and did swift mental calculations. His party would be over in four hours. In four days' time Hubert's party would come, and that would last about four hours, and then, *then*, THEN they could jolly well look out for themselves. The right hand that was clenched tightly in his coat for safety's sake was itching to plant itself firmly in Hubert's smug and smiling face. Mrs Brown, of course, was deceived by their show of friendliness.

'There, William,' she whispered triumphantly, 'I knew it would be all right. They're so nice really, and *so* grateful to you for asking them. I'm sure you'll be the *greatest* friends after this. His mother *said* that he was a nice little boy.'

William did not reply to this because there wasn't

anything that he could trust himself to say. He was still restraining himself with great difficulty from hurling himself upon his foes. They went in to tea.

'Oh, I say, how *ripping*! How *topping*!' said the Hubert Laneites gushingly to Mrs Brown, nudging each other and sniggering whenever her eye was turned away from them. Once Hubert looked at William and made his most challenging grimace, turning immediately to Mrs Brown to say with an ingratiating smile, 'It's a simply topping party, Mrs Brown, and it's awfully nice of you to ask us.'

Mrs Brown beamed at him and said, 'It's so nice to *have* you, Hubert,' and the other Hubert Laneites sniggered, and William kept his hands in his pockets with such violence that one of them went right through the lining. But the crowning catastrophe happened when they pulled the crackers.

Hubert went up to William, and said, 'See what I've got out of a cracker, William,' and held up a ring that sent a squirt of water into William's face. The Hubert Laneites went into paroxysms of silent laughter. Hubert was all smirking contrition.

'I say, I'm so sorry, William, I'd no idea that it would do

that. I'm frightfully sorry, Mrs Brown. I'd no idea that it would do that. I just got it out of one of the crackers. I say, I'm *so* sorry, William.'

It was evident to everyone but Mrs Brown that the ring had not come out of a cracker, but had been carefully brought by Hubert in order to play this trick on William. William was wiping water out of his eyes and ears.

'It's quite all right, dear,' said Mrs Brown. 'It was *quite* an accident, we all saw. They shouldn't have such nasty things in crackers, but it wasn't your fault. Tell him that you don't mind a bit, William.'

But William hastily left the room.

'Now let's go and have a few games, shall we?' said Mrs Brown.

Ginger followed William upstairs, and found him on the hearthrug in his bedroom, kneeling over a bolster that he was violently pummelling. Ginger knew that to William the bolster was not the bolster, but Hubert Lane's plump, well-nourished body. William raised a shining purple face from his task, and then the glow faded from it as he realised that the prostrate form before him was merely the bolster, and that Hubert Lane was triumphantly sniggering among his friends downstairs, not yet overtaken by Nemesis.

'Why don't you go down and show him?' said Ginger simply.

William, returning reluctantly to Reality, raised the limp form of the bolster, and threw it on to the bed.

'Can't,' he said tersely. 'Can't do anything not while he's in our house. I—'

'William, darling,' called his mother. 'Come down, we're going to begin the games.'

William and Ginger went downstairs, and the rest of the party passed off uneventfully. The Hubert Laneites said goodbye at the end with nauseous gratitude, and went sniggering down the drive.

'*There*, William!' said Mrs Brown, as she shut the door. 'I knew it would be all right. They were so grateful and they enjoyed it *so* much and you're *quite* friends now, aren't you?'

But William was already upstairs in his bedroom pummelling his bolster with such energy that he burst his collar open. During the days that intervened between William's party and Hubert Lane's party, the Hubert Laneites kept carefully out of the way of the Outlaws. Yet the Outlaws felt uneasily that something was brewing. Not content with scoring over them at William's party, Hubert meant to score over them in some way at his own. The Hubert Laneites looked upon the truce, not as something that tied their hands for the time being, but as something that delivered their enemies into their power. William was uneasily aware that Hubert Lane would not feel the compunction that he had felt in the matter of his guests.

'We've gotter do somethin' to them at their party, same as they did to us at ours,' said Ginger firmly.

'Yes, but what can we do?' said William. 'We can't start fightin' 'em. We've promised not to. An' – an' there's nothin' else we *can* do. Jus' wait, jus' *wait* till their party's over.'

'But they'll never forget that water squirt,' said Ginger mournfully.

'Unless we do somethin' back,' said Douglas.

'What *can* we do in *their* house with them watchin' us all the time?' said Henry.

'We mus' jus' *think*,' said William, 'there's four days an' we'll think hard.'

But the day of Hubert's party arrived, and they'd thought

of nothing. William looked downcast and spiritless. Even pummelling his bolster had lost its charm for him.

They met in the old barn in the morning to arrange their plan of action, but none of them could think of any plan of action to arrange, and the meeting broke up gloomily at lunch time, without having come to any decision at all.

William walked slowly and draggingly through the village on his way home. His mother had told him to stop at the baker's with an order for her, and it was a sign of his intense depression that he remembered to do it. In ordinary circumstances William forgot his mother's messages in the village. He entered the baker's shop and stared around him resentfully. It seemed to be full of people. He'd have to wait all night before anyone took any notice of him. Just his luck, he reflected bitterly . . . Then he suddenly realised that the mountainous lady just in front of him was Mrs Lane. She was talking in a loud voice to a friend.

'Yes, Hubie's party is this afternoon. We're having William Brown and his friends. To put a stop to that silly quarrel that's gone on so long, you know. Hubie's so lovable that I simply can't think how anyone could quarrel with him. But, of course, it will be all right after today. We're having a Father Christmas, you know. Bates, our gardener, is going to be Father Christmas and give out presents. I've given Hubie three pounds to get some *really* nice presents for it to celebrate the ending of the feud.'

William waited his turn, gave his message, and went home for lunch.

Immediately after lunch he made his way to Bates's cottage.

It stood on the road at the end of the Lanes' garden. One gate led from the garden to the road, and the other from the garden to the Lanes' shrubbery. Behind the cottage was Bates's treasured kitchen garden, and at the bottom was a little shed where he stored his apples. The window of the shed had to be open for airing purposes, but Bates kept a sharp look out for his perpetual and inveterate enemies, boys.

William approached the cottage with great circumspection, looking anxiously around to be sure that none of the Hubert Laneites was in sight. He had reckoned on the likelihood of their all being engaged in preparation for the party.

He opened the gate, walked up the path, and knocked

at the door, standing poised on one foot ready to turn to flee should Bates, recognising him and remembering some of his former exploits in his kitchen garden, attack him on sight. He heaved a sigh of relief, however, when Bates opened the door. It was clear that Bates did not recognise him. He received him with an ungracious scowl, but that, William could see, was because he was *a* boy, not because he was *the* boy.

'Well?' said Bates sharply, holding the door open a few inches. 'What d'you want?'

William assumed an ingratiating smile, the smile of a boy who has every right to demand admittance to the cottage.

'I say,' he said with a fairly good imitation of the Hubert Laneites' most patronising manner, 'you've got the Father Christmas things here, haven't you?'

The ungraciousness of Bates's scowl did not relax, but he opened the door a few inches wider in a resigned fashion. He had been pestered to death over the Father Christmas things. These boys had been in and out of his cottage all day with parcels and what not, trampling over his doorstep and 'mussing up' everything. He'd decided some time ago that it wasn't going to be worth the five shillings that Mrs Lane was giving him for it. He took for granted that William was one of the Hubert Laneites coming once more to 'muss up' his bag of parcels, and take one out or put one in, or snigger over them as they'd been doing every day for the last week. But he *did* think that they'd have left him in peace on the very afternoon of the party.

'Yes,' he said surlily, 'I've got the things 'ere an' they're all right, so there's no call to start upsettin' of 'em again. I've had enough of you comin' in an' mussin' the place up.'

'I only wanted to count them, and make sure that we've got the right number,' said William with an oily friendliness that was worthy of Hubert himself.

The man opened the door with a shrug.

'All right,' he said, 'go in and count 'em. I tell you, I'm sick of the whole lot of you, I am. Mussin' the place up. Look at your boots!'

William looked at his boots, made an ineffectual attempt to wipe them on the mat, and entered the cottage. He had an exhilarating sense of danger and adventure as he entered. At any minute he might arouse the man's suspicions. His ignorance of where the presents were, for instance, when he was supposed to have been visiting them regularly, might give him away completely. Moreover, a Hubert Laneite might arrive any minute and trap him, in the cottage. It was, in short, a situation after William's own heart. The immediate danger of discovery was averted by Bates himself, who waved him irascibly into the back parlour, where the presents were evidently kept. William entered, and threw a quick glance out of the window. Yes, Ginger was there, as they had arranged he should be, hovering near the shed where the apples were stored. Then he looked round the room. A red cloak and hood and white beard were spread out on the sofa, and on the hearthrug lay a sackful of small parcels.

'Well, count 'em for goodness' sake an' let's get a bit of peace,' said Bates more irritably than ever. William fell on his knees and began to make a pretence of counting the parcels. Suddenly he looked up and gazed out of the window.

'I say!' he said. 'There's a boy taking your apples.'

Bates leapt to the window. There, upon the roof of the shed, was Ginger, with an arm through the open window, obviously in the act of purloining apples and carefully exposing himself to view.

With a yell of fury Bates sprang to the door and down the path towards the shed. He had forgotten everything but this outrage upon his property. Left alone, William turned his attention quickly to the sack. It contained parcels, each one labelled and named. He had to act quickly. Bates had set off after Ginger, but he might return at any minute. Ginger's instructions were to lure him on by keeping just out of reach, but Bates might tire of the chase before they'd gone a few yards, and, remembering his visitor, return to the cottage in order to prevent his 'mussin'' things up any more than necessary. William had no time to investigate. He had to act solely upon his suspicions and his knowledge of the characters of Hubert and his friends. Quickly he began to change the labels of the little parcels, putting the one marked William on to the one marked Hubert, and exchanging the labels of the Outlaws and their supporters for those of the Hubert Laneites and their supporters. Just as he was fastening the last one, Bates returned, hot and breathless.

'Did you catch him?' said William, secure in the knowledge that Ginger had outstripped Bates more times than any of them could remember.

'Naw,' said Mr Bates, panting and furious. 'I'd like to wring his neck. I'd larn him if I got hold of him. Who was he? Did you see?'

'He was about the same size as me,' said William in the bright, eager tone of one who is trying to help, 'or he may have been just a *tiny* bit smaller.'

Bates turned upon him, as if glad of the chance to vent his irascibility upon somebody.

'Well, you clear out,' he said. 'I've had enough of you mussin' the place up, an' you can tell the others that they can keep away too. An' I'll be glad when it's over, I tell you. I'm sick of the lot of you.'

Smiling the patronising smile that he associated with the Hubert Laneites, William took a hurried departure, and ran home as quickly as he could. He found his mother searching for him despairingly.

'Oh, William, where *have* you been? You ought to have begun to get ready for the party *hours* ago.'

'I've just been for a little walk,' said William casually. 'I'll be ready in time all right.'

With the unwelcome aid of his mother, he was ready in time, spick and span and spruce and shining.

'I'm so *glad* that you're friends now and that that silly quarrel's over,' said Mrs Brown as she saw him off. 'You feel much *happier* now that you're friends, don't you?'

William snorted sardonically, and set off down the road.

The Hubert Laneites received the Outlaws with even more nauseous friendliness than they had shown at William's house. It was evident, however, from the way they sniggered and nudged each other that they had some plan prepared. William felt anxious. Suppose that the plot they had so obviously prepared had nothing to do with the Father Christmas . . . Suppose that he had wasted his time and trouble that morning . . .

They went into the hall after tea, and Mrs Lane said roguishly, 'Now, boys, I've got a visitor for you.' Immediately Bates, inadequately disguised as Father Christmas and looking fiercely resentful of the whole proceedings, entered with his sack. The Hubert Laneites sniggered delightedly. This was evidently the crowning moment of the afternoon. Bates took the parcels out one by one, announcing the name on each label.

The first was William.

The Hubert Laneites watched him go up to receive it in

paroxysms of silent mirth. William took it and opened it, wearing a sphinx-like expression. It was the most magnificent mouth organ that he had ever seen. The mouths of the Hubert Laneites dropped open in horror and amazement. It was evidently the present that Hubert had destined for himself. Bates called out Hubert's name. Hubert, his mouth still hanging open with horror and amazement, went to receive his parcel. It contained a short pencil with shield and rubber of the sort that can be purchased for a penny or twopence. He went back to his seat blinking. He examined his label. It bore his name. He examined William's label. It bore his name. There was no mistake about it. William was thanking Mrs Lane effusively for his present.

'Yes, dear,' she was saying, 'I'm so glad you like it. I haven't had time to look at them but I told Hubie to get nice things.'

Hubert opened his mouth to protest, and then shut it again. He was beaten and he knew it. He couldn't very well tell his mother that he'd spent the bulk of the money on the presents for himself and his particular friends, and had spent only a few coppers on the Outlaws' presents. He couldn't think what had happened. He'd been so sure that it

BATES CALLED OUT THE NAMES ONE BY ONE.
THE FIRST WAS WILLIAM.

IT WAS THE MOST MAGNIFICENT MOUTH ORGAN
THAT HE HAD EVER SEEN. THE HUBERT LANEITES
STARED IN HORROR AND AMAZEMENT.

would be all right. The Outlaws would hardly have had the nerve publicly to object to their presents, and Mrs Lane was well meaning but conveniently short sighted, and took for granted that everything that Hubie did was perfect. Hubert sat staring at his pencil and blinking his eyes in incredulous horror. Meanwhile the presentation was going on. Bertie Franks's present was a ruler that could not have cost more than a penny, and Ginger's was a magnificent electric torch. Bertie stared at the torch with an expression that would have done credit to a tragic mask, and Ginger hastened to establish his permanent right to his prize by going up to thank Mrs Lane for it.

'Yes, it's lovely, dear,' she said. 'I told Hubert to get nice things.'

Douglas's present was a splendid penknife, and Henry's a fountain pen, while the corresponding presents for the Hubert Laneites were an india-rubber and a notebook. The Hubert Laneites watched their presents passing into the enemies' hands with expressions of helpless agony. But Douglas's parcel had more than a penknife in it. It had a little bunch of imitation flowers with an india-rubber bulb attached and a tiny label, 'Show this to William and press the rubber thing'. Douglas took it to Hubert. Hubert knew it, of course, for he had bought it, but he was paralysed with horror at the whole situation.

'Look, Hubert,' said Douglas.

A fountain of ink caught Hubert neatly in the eye. Douglas was all surprise and contrition.

'I'm so sorry, Hubert,' he said. 'I'd no idea that it was going to do that. I've just got it out of my parcel and I'd no idea that it was going to do that. I'm so sorry, Mrs Lane, I'd no idea that it was going to do that.'

'Of course you hadn't, dear,' said Mrs Lane. 'It's Hubie's own fault for buying a thing like that. It's very foolish of him indeed.'

Hubert wiped the ink out of his eyes and sputtered helplessly.

Then William discovered that it was time to go.

'Thank you so much for our lovely presents, Hubert,' he said politely. 'We've had a *lovely* time.'

And Hubert, under his mother's eye, smiled a green and sickly smile.

The Outlaws marched triumphantly down the road, brandishing their spoils. William was playing on his mouth organ, Ginger was flashing his electric light, Henry waving his fountain pen, and Douglas slashing at the hedge with his penknife.

Occasionally they turned round to see if their enemies were pursuing them, in order to retrieve their treasures.

But the Hubert Laneites were too broken in spirit to enter into open hostilities just then.

As they walked, the Outlaws raised a wild and inharmonious paean of triumph.

And over the telephone Mrs Lane was saying to Mrs Brown, 'Yes, dear, it's been a *complete* success. They're the *greatest* friends now. I'm sure it's been a Christmas that they'll all remember all their lives.'

CHAPTER 8

WILLIAM'S CHRISTMAS EVE

William wandered slowly down the road. It was Christmas Eve, but the rush of preparation for Christmas was over. The presents he had prepared for his relations were safely wrapped up and put away in readiness for tomorrow. He had secretly discovered, examined and approved the presents that his relations had bought for him. There was nothing to do but to enjoy the afternoon, and he had arranged to do this by joining the Outlaws at a game of Cops and Robbers in the woods.

He walked along whistling and swinging a stick he had taken from the hedgerows. But he was not thinking about the Outlaws or the game of Cops and Robbers. He was thinking of Diana, the little girl who had recently arrived to live at the Hall with her father, Major Blake. She had shown distinct signs of favour to William, and the thought of her was beginning to come between him and his normal pursuits. As he walked along now, he was imagining that he met her at the bend of the road, that she stopped and talked to him, that she asked him to tea . . .

He turned the bend of the road – and ran into her so violently that he almost knocked her down. She was not alone, however. She was with the tall, elderly, aristocratic-looking aunt who had arrived yesterday to spend Christmas at the Hall.

William apologised profusely. Diana smiled at him sweetly. The aunt looked down her aristocratic nose.

'This is William,' said Diana.

'How do you do?' said the aunt, holding out an aristocratic hand.

'Very well, thank you,' said William, placing his grimy hand within it.

The aunt took out a handkerchief and carefully wiped a smear of mud from her grey kid gloves.

They passed on. Diana darted back.

'William,' she whispered, 'come round to the Hall's quick as you can. I'll be in the shrubbery. I want you to do something for me.'

William's heart expanded in a warm glow of knight-errantry. At last his dreams were coming true. She wanted him to do something for her . . .

He imagined himself killing dragons for her, fighting a thousand robbers single-handed, putting to flight hordes of savage beasts. He was in the act of slaying an imaginary dragon in the middle of the road when the other Outlaws came upon him. Somewhat sheepishly he abandoned his pugnacious attitude and picked up the stick with which he had just lunged at the invisible beast.

'What are you doing?' inquired Ginger.

'Jus' walkin' along,' replied William coldly.

'Well, come on an' play Cops and Robbers.'

'I can't,' said William. 'I'm afraid I'm busy this afternoon.'

'But you said you were coming.'

'Well, I've changed my mind,' said William. 'I'm busy.'

'Where are you going?'

'Never mind,' said William. 'I'm busy.'

He walked on. Sadly they watched him turn into the field path that led to the Hall shrubbery.

'Cops and Robbers is no fun without him,' said Henry.

'It's that girl,' said Ginger, shaking his head gloomily. 'It's that girl.'

They walked slowly on towards the woods. William, too, walked on a little more soberly. The meeting with the Outlaws had brought his soaring imagination back to earth. He realised that Diana could not possibly want him to kill a dragon or fight robbers and wild beasts. He realised this with regret, for he had always felt that he would distinguish himself in such contests.

He reached the shrubbery and waited there patiently, concealed in the bushes. After some time Diana returned from her walk with her aunt and joined him.

'Oh, *there* you are, William. I'm so glad. I *knew* you'd come.'

The note of admiration in her voice was gratifying.

'*Course* I'd come,' he said, swaggering as well as he could, considering that he was closely hemmed in by laurel bushes on all sides. 'What d'you want me to do? I bet there's no one in the world I can't fight.'

'Oh, I don't want you to fight anyone, William,' she said.

His face fell. Even though it couldn't be dragons or wild

beasts, he'd rather hoped it might be Hubert Lane or Bertie Franks or one of their gang.

'What d'you want me to do, then?' he said.

She drew nearer and sank her voice to a confidential whisper.

'OH, *THERE* YOU ARE, WILLIAM. I'M SO GLAD.'

'Listen,' she said. 'It's Aunt Alex's Christmas present to me. It's a doll. I found it in one of her drawers, tied up in a parcel with "To my dear little niece" written on it. And I *hate* dolls. I wanted a train.'

William looked at her, bewildered. 'Yes, but what can I do?' he said.

'I want you to steal it,' said Diana. 'Then she'll find it gone tomorrow, and it'll be too late to buy anything else, so she'll have to give me money, and I'll buy the train myself.'

He gaped at her.

'But—' he began.

She interrupted him.

'I can't steal it. She'd be sure to see me coming out of her room with it. Or somebody would. Besides, I don't like telling really big stories, and it would be a really big story to say I didn't know anything about it if I'd done it myself, and it would only be a little story to say I didn't know anything about it if you'd done it.'

William considered this point of view. There was certainly something to be said for it. Still – he looked up without enthusiasm at the enormous fortress-like house into which he was expected to make a felonious entrance –

he'd far rather have fought someone . . .

'Tell you what,' he suggested at last. 'You go up an' get it and throw it out of the window to me, an' I'll take it away.'

Diana shook her head.

'No,' she said slowly. 'I don't want to do anything myself. You see, I want to pretend to myself that I don't know anything about it, and of course I can't do that if I've thrown it out of the window to you.'

'No, I suppose you can't,' said William, once more turning his eye upon the stately mansion and wishing it had been a dragon. 'Well, how can I get it?'

'It's quite easy,' said Diana. 'You can go up that fire-escape staircase to the room at the corner there – the one with the green curtains. That's her sitting-room, and the bedroom's next door to it. The present's in the drawer in the wardrobe. It's a square parcel with "To my dear little niece" written on it. You must get it and go back to the sitting-room and come down the fire-escape again. It's quite easy.'

'Y-yes,' agreed William doubtfully. 'Er – s'pose she's in her sitting-room.'

'She won't be,' said Diana. 'And if she is you can hide behind the curtains. They're long curtains that come right down to the ground.'

'Y-yes,' said William again, still more doubtfully. 'Y-yes. An' s'pose she comes into the bedroom while I'm getting it.'

'You must just make a dash for it,' said Diana. 'It's quite easy. Of course,' – her manner became rather chilly – 'if you're *afraid* . . .'

'I'm not afraid,' said William indignantly. 'At least,' as the memory of the tall, elderly, aristocratic-looking aunt returned to him, 'I'm not afraid of robbers or wild beasts or that sort of thing. I say,' he continued, after a thoughtful pause, 'what's your aunt like when she's angry?'

'She's awful,' said Diana darkly. '*Awful*. But don't worry. She won't catch you if you're quick.'

'No, of course not,' said William, and repeated, as if to reassure himself, 'Of course not.' After another thoughtful pause he continued, 'P'raps I'd better not do it. For your sake, I mean,' he added hastily. 'I mean, if she catches me you'll get into a row for setting me on to it.'

Diana looked at him with large surprised eyes.

'Oh, no, I won't,' she assured him. 'I shall say that I'd

no idea that you were going to do it, and even if you say I told you to do it I shall say I didn't. Because, you see, I'm pretending to myself that I don't know anything about it. So you needn't be afraid of me getting into a row.'

'N-no,' said William, and, in spite of the removal of this anxiety, he looked strangely despondent. 'N-no. I'm jolly glad about that, of course.' Again he considered deeply and finally remarked, 'You know it might be an awfully nice doll.'

'I hate dolls.'

'Yes, but I mean, if you tried playing with this one you might like it. Lots of girls do like dolls, you know.'

Again she looked at him coldly.

'If you don't want to do a little thing like this for me . . .' she said, and added reproachfully, 'I thought you liked me.'

'I do,' said William earnestly. 'Honest, I do.' The coldness and reproach of the little girl's glance spurred him on to superhuman daring. 'I'll go 'n' get it now. Just watch me. I'll be done with it in two shakes.'

Without waiting to consider, he hurried through the shrubbery, up the fire-escape, and in at the open window where the green curtains swayed in the breeze. Then he drew a deep breath and looked about him. It was a pleasant, fair-sized sitting-room, fortunately empty. From it a door led into the next room, which was presumably the bedroom. William, still upheld by his impulse of daring, was just making his way across the room to this door when he heard the sound of voices approaching and the handle of the door was turned. Swift as lightning he returned to the shelter of the curtains and stood concealed behind them. The aunt entered, accompanied by her Pekinese and a visitor.

'Yes,' said the aunt, 'it's a nice little room. A nice view, too.'

They came over to the window and stood so close to William that he thought they must hear his heart beating.

Then they went to sit by the fire, leaving William in peace. But the peace was short-lived, for almost immediately the Pekinese discovered William's feet, which protruded from the bottom of the curtain. He fell upon them with a ferocious growl and began to worry them. William managed with difficulty to strangle the 'Ow!' that was his natural reaction to this proceeding. The growls grew louder.

'What's the matter with Peky?' said the visitor.

The aunt threw a careless glance over her shoulder.

'Oh, he must have found his india-rubber bone. He'll worry it like that by the hour, the darling!'

They returned to their conversation, and the Pekinese to his self-imposed task of tearing the socks from William's skin, and the skin from his ankles. William had reached the point at which discovery was preferable to further torture, when the aunt and the visitor rose and went out, the aunt calling 'Peky!' over her shoulder.

William had the satisfaction of getting in a fairly good kick at his tormentor as it departed reluctantly, still snarling defiance at the two strange intruders who had appeared so unexpectedly beneath the curtain.

William heaved a sigh of relief as the door closed on them. The coast was clear at last. But the episode had shaken his nerve and destroyed the first fine careless rapture of bravado in which he had undertaken the adventure. He stayed for some minutes in the window embrasure, trying once more to screw up his courage to make the dash for the bedroom. He had just managed to screw it up – partially, at any rate – when he heard the sounds of the aunt and visitor returning, accompanied by the Pekinese. The aunt and the visitor he might have endured, but the thought of the Pekinese, who would, of course, immediately seek out again his late victims, completed the breaking of his nerve, and he climbed lightly out of the window, and proceeded farther up the fire-escape. It led to an open window which he regarded hopefully till he caught a glimpse of a maid arranging her cap before a mirror. He hurried on and found himself upon the roof.

It was a much-gabled roof, and he decided to explore it while he had the opportunity. He had reached the summit of the first gable when he was startled by the sound of voices and realised that the aunt and visitor had come out on to the balcony. He froze rigid on his gable.

'Yes, I really ought to have shown you the view from here,' the aunt was saying. 'It's a wonderful view.'

'Wonderful,' agreed the visitor vaguely. She gazed round till her eyes finally rested upon William. 'What a quaint old gargoyle up there on the roof!' she commented. 'I'm short-sighted, of course, but to me from here it looks a delightfully quaint piece of work.'

William hastily slid down from his gable-point to a hollow of the roof. The aunt found her *lorgnettes* and slowly turned them on to the gable.

'No, dear,' she said at last. 'It's just a tree-top that you see.'

'I suppose so,' said the friend in rather a perplexed fashion. 'Of course, I *am* very short-sighted . . . It certainly seems to have gone from where it was.'

'It's a tree-top moving in the wind,' explained the aunt.

They disappeared into the house. So shattered was William's nerve by this time that, though he had by no means abandoned the enterprise, he decided not to return to the fire-escape, but to try to make a less obtrusive entrance from the roof. After clambering about for some time he discovered a chimney that seemed to be large and smokeless and accommodating. He was just peering into it hopefully when a gust of sooty smoke caught him in the face. He withdrew, choking. Someone had evidently just lit the fire. He continued his exploration till he came to a skylight. He opened it and began to let himself down gently into the room below, receiving somewhat of a shock as he felt his legs dangling into a tank of ice-cold water. He wriggled away from it and at last dropped on to the ground clear of it, bruising himself considerably in the process. Limping slightly from the combined effect of the Pekinese and the fall, he went along a passage and down a staircase. Fortune seemed suddenly to favour him, for the staircase led to the landing just outside the sitting-room with the green curtains.

He darted into it and through the door into the bedroom. He opened the drawer, found the parcel, and dashed back into the sitting-room. Unfortunately a maid had just come in to put coals on the fire. She gazed at the limping apparition, then gave a yell and fled. William slipped down the fire-escape, still clutching his parcel, and joined the little girl in the shrubbery.

'Oh, William, how *dreadful* you look!' she greeted him with distaste.

'Can't help it,' panted William. 'It was a chimney and a water-tank . . . Here's the parcel.'

She took it, and a smile of triumph dawned slowly on her face.

'Oh, William, *thank* you,' she said. 'I *knew* you'd get it . . . and I've got a reward for you. I've asked aunt if you may come to tea, and she says you may. But you look *awful*, William. You'll have to get tidy, or I know she won't let you stay to tea. And the parcel . . . she mustn't find that. What'll we do with it?'

'*I* know,' said William. 'Our gardner's got a fire. I'll go home an' burn it an' get tidy for comin' to tea with you.'

'Oh, *yes*, William,' said the little girl eagerly. 'Oh, William, you are *clever*. And you are brave, too. I shall never forget how you went straight up the fire-escape to get that parcel.'

THE MAID GAVE A YELL AND FLED.

'Oh, that's nothin',' murmured William complacently. 'Nothin' at all.'

'Well, you'd better be quick, William,' urged Diana. 'It would be *awful* if aunt caught you all wet like that, and with the parcel.'

Realising this, William set off homeward as quickly as possible.

In about half an hour he returned, still limping, but spick and span and without the parcel.

'I've burnt it,' he said. 'I've burnt it till there wasn't anything at all of it left. An' I've made myself jolly tidy, haven't I?'

'Yes, you *have*,' said the little girl admiringly. 'William, I think you're *wonderful*!'

At this moment the aunt issued from the front door and came across the lawn to them. She was carrying a large parcel under her arm.

'Is this the little friend you're having to tea?' she asked.

'Yes,' said Diana.

The aunt looked at William rather coldly.

'Well, don't get rough,' she said. 'I'll be back by tea-time, but I just have to go to the post office.' She turned to Diana. 'I hope you don't mind, dear. I'm afraid I shall have to send the train I'd got for you to your little cousin Dorita. I'd got a doll for her, but when I went to look for it just now it wasn't there. I suppose I must have forgotten to bring it. So I'm sending her your train. I'm sure you won't mind, dear, will you? I've got a nice book that I know you'd like instead. Stories from English History. I can't send that to Dorita because I sent it to her last year. But I'm certain you'll like it, and won't grudge her your train. And you'll play quietly till I come back, won't you?'

She swept on down the drive. There was a tense silence.

Then the little girl turned on William, her small face pink with anger.

'It's all your fault, you hateful boy! You took it and burnt it, and now I've got to have a rotten old history book instead of my train . . . I *hate* you.'

William blinked at her in amazement.

'B-b-but you told me to,' he stammered.

The little girl stamped her foot.

'Don't keep *arguing* about it,' she stormed. 'It's *all* your fault. You burnt the doll, and so I've got to have a rotten old history book instead of my train. I hope someone burns up all your presents like you've burnt up mine. And go away. I don't want you. I don't ever want to see you again as long as I live . . .'

The Outlaws, engaged in a not very successful game of Cops and Robbers – for no game seemed fully successful when William was not there – were surprised and secretly relieved to see William coming through the wood to join them. He still limped slightly and looked tidier than usual, though already a good deal of the spick-and-spanness achieved for his visit to the little girl had fallen from him.

'Hello,' said Ginger. 'Have you hurt your foot?'

'No,' said William.

'Thought you weren't coming,' said Douglas.

William assumed an expression of rather cold surprise.

'Not coming?' he said. 'Why shouldn't I be coming?'

'I thought you were going to that girl.'

'What girl?' countered William.

'Diana Blake,' said Ginger.

William appeared to search deeply in his memory.

'Oh, *that* girl,' he said, as if a faint memory had emerged

'IT'S ALL YOUR FAULT,' DIANA STORMED.
'I DON'T EVER WANT TO SEE YOU AGAIN AS LONG AS I LIVE.'

from the far distant past. '*That* girl. Good gracious, no! I've finished with her for ever. I've finished with all girls for ever . . . Come on. Let's start playing Cops and Robbers.'

CHAPTER 9

A PRESENT FROM WiLLiAM

'The part about Christmas I don't like,' said Ginger, 'is having so many relations round. I never did care much for relations.'

'Aunts are the worst,' said William with a sigh. 'Always making such a fuss about nothin' at all, jus' 'cause you make a quiet noise on a trumpet or somethin' like that. We had one last year that said my mouth organ went right through her head. Stands to reason it couldn't've done. I s'pose she'd got a solid head same as everyone else. Then a pea out of my catapult hit her once by mistake an' she said it had given her a nervous breakdown. She was jolly awful. Thank goodness we aren't having any this year. They asked the same aunt again an' she said that if I was going to be at home she'd rather not come, thank you. An' I jolly well feel the same way about her.'

'We're having one,' said Ginger gloomily. 'A sort of cousin.'

'Cousins aren't as bad as aunts,' said William.

'This one will be. She's a sort of a second cousin, an' she's older than my mother. An' she's bringing a cat.'

'I had one that brought a cat once,' said William gloomily. 'It was an awful cat. It got mad whenever you tried to teach it tricks. An' *she* got mad whenever you looked at it. I tried to get it to make friends with Jumble jus' out of kindness 'cause I wanted it to have a friend, an' she told my mother I'd been setting my dog on it. Jumble had only jus' bitt'n a bit of its fur off jus' playin' with it, an' she set up such a fuss you'd have thought I'd murdered it. Aunts are jolly bad, anyway, but the ones that have cats are the worst.'

'It's goin' to be a rotten Christmas for me,' said Ginger. 'I've not got any money to buy people Christmas presents with.'

'Nor have I,' said Henry.

'Nor have I,' said Douglas.

'I've not had any money for so long,' said William

pathetically, 'that I've almost forgotten what it feels like to have money.'

'They *say* it's the thought that matters, not the acshul present,' said Ginger, 'but I've noticed that they're jolly sniffy when you give 'em the thought an' not the acshul present.'

'An' they *say* that they'd rather you took a little trouble makin' them things than jus' buyin' them, an' when you do they start makin' an awful fuss. I made a jolly nice plant pot for a Christmas present once out of an old hat of Ethel's, only it turned out it wasn't an old hat, an' everyone was mad with me. Every time I've ever tried to make anything for anyone it's only made them mad with me, so I'm jolly well not goin' to do it any more. Funny how we never seem to have any money at Christmas! An' no one ever gives us any for presents, only ties an' books an' pencil boxes an' things like that.'

'I'd like to be able to give my mother somethin' nice,' said Ginger wistfully.

The others agreed. They all would have liked to be able to give their mothers something nice . . .

'I bet mine would give me a bit of money for it if I asked

her,' said Douglas, 'but it doesn't seem right gettin' the money from the person you want to buy the present for.'

The others agreed. It certainly didn't seem right.

'Next year I'm jolly well goin' to start savin' up for presents weeks an' *weeks* before Christmas.'

The others agreed. They agreed every year . . .

'It's Guy Fawkes' day that throws it all wrong,' said Henry bitterly. 'You use up all the money you've got an' all the money you're goin' to have for weeks on fireworks, an' then you've got to pay for all the windows an' things that get broke by the fireworks, an' by the time Christmas comes you've no money at all. I think that there ought to be a lor puttin' Guy Fawkes' day in the middle of summer, then it'd give you time to get over it an' have a bit of money by Christmas.'

They agreed. They agreed every year . . .

'What about this sort of cousin that's comin' to you for Christmas?' said William hopefully to Ginger. 'P'raps she'll give us a tip or somethin'.'

'No, she won't,' said Ginger. 'She hasn't got any money. She's poor. She's a sort of housekeeper to someone. She went to keep house for an ole uncle what was supposed to be rich an' then when he died it turned out that he hadn't any money, an' so she had to go out to work.'

They considered the picture without enthusiasm.

'Doesn't sound as if *she'd* be much use,' said William finally. 'We shall jus' have to think of some way.'

Ginger's mother's second cousin arrived that evening, and Ginger met the Outlaws after supper to report.

'I s'pose she's *awful*,' they said morosely.

'N-no,' said Ginger, 'she's not bad. Come round an' have a look at her tomorrow.'

They arrived the next day to inspect her and found her small and thin and grey-haired and eager.

'I'm so glad to meet Ginger's friends,' she said. 'I've got some sweets for you all in my bag.'

She was shy and deprecating and quite unlike any elderly female relative they had ever met. They liked her at once.

'And I must show you my cat,' she went on. 'He belonged to my Uncle Josiah when I used to keep house for him, and when he died my uncle had him stuffed and left him to me in his will.'

Their interest rose when they heard that the cat was not a real cat. William was interested in stuffed animals. He

'I'M SO GLAD TO MEET GINGER'S FRIENDS,' SHE SAID.

had once tried without much success to stuff a dead rat.

She took them up to her bedroom and showed them a stuffed cat that sat on the chair by her bed. It was a large, sleek-looking animal, with glass eyes that seemed to hold a sinister gleam.

'Poor puss!' said Miss Carrol, putting her hand upon the sleek black head. 'My uncle was bedridden and puss used to sit by his bedside, looking at him for hours. They seemed to be talking to each other, and my uncle would chuckle and puss always seemed to chuckle back. I didn't really like poor puss, I'm afraid. There seemed to be something so uncanny about him. Pluto, my uncle called him. Such a heathenish name! Then he died, and my uncle had him stuffed and put on the chair by his bed, and no one else ever had to sit on that chair. He still used to chuckle at him, and puss still seemed to chuckle back. And he left puss to me in his will, and so I've had him ever since. I try to set as much store by him as uncle did, because I feel it's all I can do for his memory. It seems silly to bring him away with me, but somehow, when I think how uncle couldn't bear him out of his sight, I don't feel it right to leave him alone at home for Christmas, poor puss, and I've got quite fond of him now, in a way.'

The stuffed cat fascinated the Outlaws. They liked to go up to Miss Carrol's bedroom and look at it and hear stories about Miss Carrol's Uncle Josiah. He seemed to have been an odd old man with a distorted, sardonic sense of humour. He loved to play unpleasant tricks on his niece – to set her looking for things in places where he knew they could not be found, to rouse her from her sleep by groans of simulated agony, to summon her up the steep narrow stairs time after time for no other purpose than to send her down again, to hide her thimble or needlework beneath his pillow and watch her hunting for them, to pull her hair or tweak her nose as she bent over him to straighten his pillow. He had not been a pleasant old man . . .

'But, still,' she excused him with her gentle smile, 'it amused him, and it didn't do me any harm. I was very sorry for him, and I've always tried to keep puss nice as he'd have liked him, with moth powder and a good brushing every day and so on.'

The Outlaws took her round the village and showed her their favourite haunts. They had her to tea in the old barn, making the tea and toast themselves over a fire of sticks. Both tea and toast had a peculiar flavour, but Miss Carrol said they were delicious. They confided their ambitions to her – Ginger's to be an engine-driver, Henry's an acrobat, Douglas's a gangster, and William's a world potentate. She confided her ambition to them – which was to own a small cottage in the country. They even found the ideal cottage for her – Honeysuckle Cottage, a little cottage covered with honeysuckle just outside the village, which happened to be To Let. In imagination they helped her to furnish and equip it.

Attracted by her shy friendliness, they told her about the presents they would like to give their mothers but couldn't afford to. With her help they chose a new travelling-clock for Ginger's mother, a silk scarf for William's, a cut-glass scent spray for Henry's, and a new leather handbag for Douglas's. They felt strangely comforted and exhilarated by the process.

'Now I'm going to rest in my cottage till supper time,' she said, 'and you must go and hide your presents carefully away so that your mothers can't find them.'

They had never met any grown-up before who entered so perfectly into the spirit of the game.

It was the next day that the idea occurred to William of

introducing Jumble to Pluto.

'I mean, jus' hold him up an' see what Jumble'll make of him. I don't mean let Jumble touch him or anything like that, but jus' see if Jumble thinks he's real. Let's go an' ask her if we can. I bet she'll let us.'

They went up to Miss Carrol's bedroom, but Miss Carrol was not there. Pluto, however, was there, sitting on the chair by the bed and wearing his usual leer. After a slight hesitation they entered and stood round the chair, gazing at him.

'I bet she wouldn't mind us jus' takin' him down an' holdin' him up for Jumble to see,' said William at last. 'It can't possibly do any harm. We won't let Jumble touch him or anything like that.'

The others agreed, and, slipping Pluto beneath his coat, William led the way down to the back garden, where Jumble awaited them. They stood in an expectant crowd, while William slowly drew Pluto from his hiding-place. Jumble cocked his head on one side and wagged his tail.

'He likes it,' said William. Very cautiously he lowered Pluto towards Jumble. Jumble stood up on his hind legs and smelled his new acquaintance with every evidence of friendliness, still wagging his tail.

'He *does* like it,' said William. 'Let's let him make friends with it properly. I bet she'd be jolly pleased to find that Jumble'd made friends with it. She likes Jumble.'

He set Pluto upon the grass and stood back to watch the obvious friendliness of Jumble's deepen into an abiding affection. Jumble approached, still wagging his tail ingratiatingly, then suddenly met the baleful stare of the sinister green eyes. It seemed to madden him. He sprang at the leering Pluto and seized him savagely by the neck. The Outlaws leapt to the rescue, but Jumble ran into the bushes with his victim, shaking and chewing him as he ran, ignoring William's threats and entreaties.

At last, realising that William was gaining on him, and feeling that the green insolent stare was now fully avenged, he dropped Pluto and ran off into the woods where he spent the rest of the day, for he knew by experience that William's anger never lasted for more than a few hours.

The Outlaws gathered round Pluto, examining him with increasing dismay. For Jumble had chewed and mauled the black neck till the head fell over limply on to one side and the green eyes seemed to gaze upward in helpless bewilderment.

The Outlaws set to work at once, but all their efforts failed to restore the head to its old uprightness. They tried string and wire, even secotine and glue, but without success. The head continued to loll limply sideways, the once sleek and glossy fur of the neck was chewed and mauled, sticky with secotine, damp with William's efforts to wash off traces of the crime. After an hour of hard work on the Outlaws' part, even William, the optimist, had to admit that Pluto looked worse than when they had begun.

'She'll be *mad*,' he said apprehensively.

'In a way I hope she will be,' said Ginger. 'It'll be worse if she's not mad than if she is.'

They broke the news to her very gently, standing before her in an abashed row and bringing out Pluto at the end of their recital from beneath William's coat. She went pale with horror when she saw him.

'Oh, *dear*!' she said. 'But, of course, it's not your fault, dear children, so you mustn't worry about it.'

It was, as Ginger had said, worse than if she'd been mad.

The incident seemed to bring the Outlaws face to face with the stern realities of life. They had spoilt Miss Carrol's stuffed cat, her only and much prized possession, they had not any Christmas presents for their mothers, they had not any money to buy Christmas presents for their mothers. The travelling-clock, the silk scarf, the cut-glass scent spray, and leather handbag, existed only in their imaginations. Depression swept over them. They became irritable, accusing each other of being responsible for their state of insolvency and the tragedy of Pluto.

'If you hadn't spent all that five shilling your aunt gave you for your birthday . . .'

'I like that. You spent as much of it as I did, anyway. What about that half-crown that man that came to tea with Ethel gave you?'

'Well, din' you all come to the fireworks I bought with that?'

'Yes, an' nearly got my brains blown out with you not knowin' how to set 'em off.'

''Scuse me, I *did* know how to set 'em off. It was the one I made myself that went off a bit too hard. I'd put a bit too much gunpowder in. An', anyway, you've not got any brains to be blown out, so you needn't worry about *that*.'

'Oh, I haven't, haven't I?'

'No, you haven't.'

'Well, let me tell you I've got a jolly sight more brains than you have.'

'Oh, you have, have you?'

'Yes, I have. An', anyway, whose dog was it went an' chewed up her cat? Some people's dogs don't seem to have any sense.'

'Oh, they don't, don't they?'

'No, they don't.'

'Well, let me tell you Jumble's a jolly fine dog. It was jolly brave of him.'

'Oh, it was brave, was it?'

'Yes, it was. He'd never seen a stuffed cat before, an' it might've been a dangerous animal for all he knew. S'pose it'd been a lion jus' goin' to spring at you, an' he'd gone for it like that an' saved your life, I s'pose you'd have said he hadn't any sense then. Huh!'

'Well, it wasn't a lion.'

'I never said it was.'

'Yes, you did.'

'I didn't.'

'You did.'

'I didn't.'

This conversation ran its course to the inevitable conclusion, and after the fight they all felt much more cheerful and separated for lunch on friendly terms. After lunch Ginger joined them in a state of obvious excitement.

'I say!' he said. 'I've got a shilling. Someone was there to lunch an' gave me a shilling. It's a sort of start, anyway, isn't it? Someone else might give us another shilling or something. Or, even if they don't, it's three-pence each. We can buy 'em *somethin'* with three-pence.'

William gazed at the shilling thoughtfully.

'Seems to me,' he said, 'that we oughter get her a new stuffed cat 'fore we buy anythin' else.'

Their faces fell.

'I bet they cost more'n a shilling,' said Ginger, 'an', anyway; I don't think you can buy 'em. I think you've got to get a dead 'un an' have it stuffed.'

'Well, I bet we can easy get a dead 'un,' said Douglas. 'We got one out of the pond last time we were fishin' an' I 'spect it's still there.'

'I don't think she wants *any* ole stuffed cat,' said Henry. 'She likes Pluto 'cause her uncle had it an' left it to her. I don't think she's jus' fond of *any* ole stuffed cat.'

William's face shone suddenly with the light of a great idea.

'I know,' he said, 'let's stuff that ole Pluto for her again. I bet it's quite easy. We'll stuff it so's it's head'll stand up same as it used to. We'll find out if there's any special sort of stuff for stuffin' cats, an' if there is we'll buy it with the shillin'. An' p'raps we'll have a bit left over for presents for our mothers.'

They looked at him doubtfully.

'I've gotter sort of idea,' said Ginger slowly, 'that it's a jolly difficult thing stuffin' animals. I don't b'lieve that jus' anyone can do it.'

'*Course* it isn't difficult,' said William. 'Stands to reason it isn't. You *jus'* stuff stuff into their skins till they're full of it same as they were when they were alive.'

'Well, what about that rat you tried to stuff once?'

'Well, it wasn't a good rat. It can't have been a good rat even when it was alive. It wasn't the right shape of a rat. This is diff'rent. Anyone can see it's a good cat. We'll jus' unstitch it an' stuff it, so's its head stands up straight, an' then stitch it up again an' it'll be a jolly nice surprise for her.'

As usual William's confidence was infectious, and the stuffing for Pluto became suddenly the simple process he described.

'Right!' said Ginger. 'Let's go'n' ask her now.'

'No, don't let's do that,' said William. 'It'd be much nicer for it to be a s'prise for her. She'd be jolly pleased comin' in suddenly an' finding him all stuffed fresh an' his head standin' up again like what it used to. It'd be much nicer to be a s'prise for her.'

'All right,' agreed Ginger. 'She's goin' out to tea this afternoon. Let's go'n' do it while she's out.'

They hung about the garden waiting till Miss Carrol had gone out, then they crept silently up to her room. Under William's arm was a bundle of old newspapers and some straw that he had found in a packing-case.

'This ought to be all right,' he said optimistically. 'I bet straw an' paper's what they use.'

Pluto still sat on the chair by Miss Carrol's bed, his head hanging dejectedly on to one side, his green eyes gleaming malevolently upward.

'Now,' said William in a business-like fashion, 'let's start on it. Come on.'

He sat down on the floor with Pluto on his knee and carefully examined him.

'Here's where it joins,' he said and, taking his penknife out of his pocket, began to hack away at the unfortunate Pluto's coat.

'I've cut its skin a bit,' he said casually, 'but I'll stitch it up all right at the end when I'm stitchin' up the rest.'

They watched him with eager if slightly apprehensive interest. William always embarked so light-heartedly upon adventures the end of which it was difficult to foresee.

Having made a large hole, he proceeded to pull out some drab-coloured stuffing and finally some screwed-up newspaper.

'There!' he said triumphantly. 'I told you they used newspaper for stuffin' animals. Stands to reason they do. Now I'll start puttin' it back a bit tighter, so it'll go right up its neck an' make its head stand up straight. I'll use the stuffin' what was in it first an' then fill up at the end with stuff I've brought. I bet she'll be jolly pleased.'

The others felt less optimistic, but they murmured vague acquiescence.

'It's jolly easy,' went on William airily as he pushed

newspaper and stuffing back into Pluto's gaping void. 'I bet I'll set up as an animal stuffer when I'm grown up. You jus' get a dead animal an' take its inside out an' stuff it up with newspaper an' suchlike. I'll start with small animals like caterpillars an' I'll go on till I've got to lions an' then elephants. I bet I'll be the best elephant stuffer in the world by the time I've finished. You only need a bit more stuffin' for an elephant than what you do for a caterpillar, that's all. It's jolly easy reely . . . There!'

He set the re-stuffed Pluto upon the hearthrug. It lurched tipsily over on to one side.

'I've not got it sittin' quite straight yet,' said William. 'I'll try'n' make it a bit flatter.'

The others stared at Pluto in growing dismay.

William had understated the case. Not only had he not got him sitting straight, but he was not straight anywhere. The head lolled even more limply than it had lolled before. The body was a sagging, shapeless mass.

'He's worse than he was,' said Ginger gloomily.

William stepped back to consider his handiwork. Something of his confidence obviously deserted him.

'Well,' he admitted thoughtfully, 'he cert'nly looks a bit

odd. I'd better do it again. I 'spect the old stuff's a bit wore out. I'll use my straw an' newspaper.'

He took out the stuffing and set to work again. By the time he had finished, the Outlaws' expressions of dismay had deepened to horror. Pluto seemed to have lost all semblance of his former self. His head dangled limply, his paws dangled limply, his body was completely shapeless. Even the sinister leer seemed to have left his eyes.

'It isn't like *anything*,' said Ginger faintly.

'It's a bit like a tea-cosy,' said Douglas.

'Let's say we've made it into a tea-cosy for her Christmas present,' suggested Henry.

'No, I'll have another shot,' said William in a rather small voice. Even William was dismayed by the results of his work. 'P'raps stuffin's not reely so easy. P'raps it's the sort of thing you've gotter learn. I wish now I'd practised a bit first an' worked up to it gradual.'

He took out the stuffing and examined Pluto's skin critically.

'I don't think it was ever a very good shaped cat even when it was alive,' he said. 'I bet I could have stuffed a good shaped cat all right.'

A Present from William

It was at this moment when William was sitting surrounded by newspaper, holding Pluto's empty and bedraggled skin in his hand, that Miss Carrol entered her bedroom. Intent upon their task, the Outlaws had forgotten the time, and their hostess had now returned from her tea-party. She stood and gazed at the scene, open-eyed with amazement. William tried to explain, but his explanation lacked the confidence and volubility that usually characterised William's explanations.

'Well, you see,' he stammered, 'we were doin' it as a sort of s'prise for you – stuffin' this ole cat, so's its head would stick up. It's taken us a bit longer than we thought. Well, we've not quite finished yet's a matter of fact. I'm jus' going to have another shot. I'm—'

His voice died away, as, looking at Pluto, he faced complete and overwhelming failure. 'We'll save up all our money – when we get any,' he went on, 'an' have it done for you by a proper stuffer.'

Miss Carrol rose to the occasion. She looked distressed and unhappy – Pluto had been her daily companion and friend for so many years – but she showed no anger. She did not even try to improve the occasion by a homily on the

'WE'LL SAVE UP ALL OUR MONEY, AND HAVE IT
DONE FOR YOU PROPERLY,' SAID WILLIAM.

sacredness of other people's possessions.

'It's quite all right, children,' she said. 'It was really very
silly of me to take him about with me as I did. No, I don't
want him stuffed at all, and it's *quite* all right. And you

MISS CARROL OPENED OUT THE OLD NEWSPAPER
AND GAVE A GASP OF AMAZEMENT.

mustn't worry about it. Now, let's clear all the mess up, shall we? What a lot of newspaper!'

'Yes,' explained William, 'some of it's what I brought to stuff it with, an' some of it was in it before. The yellow ones are what were in it before.'

Miss Carrol picked up the tight ball of ancient yellowed newspaper and opened it out. Then she gave a little gasp of amazement. For inside the tightly folded newspaper was a wad of notes – crinkled, crisp, hundred-pound notes – the whole of Uncle Josiah's missing fortune. That had been his final trick on her – to leave it to her stuffed in the cat she had always disliked.

Miss Carrol, William, Ginger, Henry and Douglas, all tense with excitement, boarded the bus for Hadley.

They were all going there on different business.

Miss Carrol was going to see the house-agent about Honeysuckle Cottage. William was going to buy his mother a silk scarf. Ginger was going to buy his mother a travelling-clock. Henry was going to buy his mother a cut-glass scent spray. Douglas was going to buy his mother a leather handbag.

It was going to be a jolly fine Christmas after all.